Newfangled Fairy Tales

BOOK #1

EDITED BY BRUCE LANSKY

Meadowbrook Press
Distributed by Simon & Schuster
New York

J
398.2
New

ISSN: 1093-5339

Publisher's ISBN: 0-88166-299-2
Simon & Schuster Ordering # 0-671-57704-2

Editor: Bruce Lansky
Editorial Coordinator: Liya Lev Oertel
Copyeditor: Christine Zuchora-Walske
Production Manager: Joe Gagne
Production Assistant: Danielle White
Cover Illustrator: Joy Allen

Published by Meadowbrook Press, 5451 Smetana Drive; Minnetonka, MN 55343

BOOK TRADE DISTRIBUTION by Simon & Schuster, a division of Simon and Schuster, Inc., 1230 Avenue of the Americas, New York, NY 10020

02 01 00 99 98   10 9 8 7 6 5 4 3 2

Printed in the United States of America

Contents

Acknowledgments

Thank you to all the young men and women
who served on a reading panel for this project:

Daniel Bauman, Thomas Bavota, Alex Bennett, Corey
Bertelsen, Elizabeth Bley, Steve Burton, Anthony Caputo,
Lindsay Chalupa, Alec Chambers, Noel Clary, Adam Cole,
Katelin Crook, Morgan Dewanz, Jenna Diaz, Dan Dischler,
Katherine Elwood, Jenny Finkle, Sara Ford, Tara Forste, Lauren
Harris, Nora Herrera, Laura Hollingsworth, Nathan
Hoogshagen, Jonathon Hunter, Alisia Irvin, Katelyn Isom,
Travis Jarzomski, Daniel Jasper, Jared Jay, Ashley Johnson,
Laura Jones, Alynn Kakuk, Molly Kreutter, Thomas Langle,
Kerri A. Larson, Jason Lawrence, Ben Leon, Joey Lercara, Tyler
Jo Lindquist, Kael Ludwig, Taylor R. Mallon, Brad Martin,
Glenn D. Melcher, Charles Miller, Ali Moeller, Toni Ann Molle,
Tim Moran, Richard Morril, Andrew Myers, Alissa Olson,
Rayna Olson, Jess Orr, Jenny Pamula, Manisha Patel, Lindsey
Patrick, Lisa Peterson, Morgan Pittman, Courtney Podvin,
Sonya Polson, Annissa Porter, Sarah Reed, Michelle Rich,
Raphael Rodriguez, Quentin Roman, Amy Romero, Jared Ross,
Jon Routh, Rayne Rule, Adam Schaal, Catherine Seidel, Kelli
Senzee, Elisabeth Smeltzer, Chad Smith, Nick Snow, Calvin
Stalvig, Ashley Stenberg, Jennifer Swanson, Bailey Thompson,
Whitney Tipton, Jamie Traut, Jennifer Unruh, Joban Vaishnav,
John Wagener, Annalee Warren, Joey Welch, Jessa Wicklund,
Cammie Williams, and Amber Zielinski

Introduction

Once upon a time when I was your age (and that was a very long time ago), my mother read me fairy tales at bedtime. And when she turned the lights out, I would wonder:

Why did the prince in "The Princess and the Pea" marry a princess who complained, obnoxiously, about a pea that was hidden under twenty mattresses? If she had been a true princess, she would have graciously thanked her hostess for a comfortable night's lodging.

Why was Jack rewarded for being so dumb as to trade a cow for a handful of beans and so dishonest as to steal the giant's golden goose and harp in "Jack and the Beanstalk"?

Why would the wolf in "Little Red Riding Hood" eat a sickly, old grandmother? Wouldn't it have been a lot easier (and a lot tastier) to eat Little Red Riding Hood and the contents of her picnic basket when he met her in the woods.

What kind of fairy would try to kill an innocent child ("Sleeping Beauty") just because she wasn't invited to a Christening? That fairy wasn't "upset"; she was homicidal.

Why were Cinderella, Snow White, Sleeping Beauty, and most other fairy tale "heroines" beautiful but helpless? Why did they always have to be rescued by a prince?

Why were the stepmothers in fairy tales, like "Cinderella" and "Snow White," always so mean and nasty? (In real life, the stepmothers I knew were very nice.)

In short, traditional fairy tales seemed ridiculous and weird to me. They had been written long ago—before the invention of blue jeans, peanut M&Ms, Clearasil, and *Star Wars*—which is why they seemed so obsolete.

Now that I'm more or less grown up, I've decided to write and collect the kind of fairy tales I would have liked when I was a kid. This book contains ten delightfully newfangled fairy tales that will turn everything you remember about fairy tales upside down. For example, you'll find:

- a prince who refuses to marry the crotchety "princess" who complains about a lumpy mattress;
- a wolf who would rather eat pizza than a sick, old grandmother;
- a clever princess who bribes a friendly dragon to throw a fight so she can marry the man she loves;
- a prince who saves Sleeping Beauty, Snow White, and Cinderella, but would rather get on with his career as a clothing designer than settle down with any of them.

The stories in this book are entirely unlike the predictable fairy tales you've read or seen on TV hundreds of times. I hope you enjoy them.

Bruce Lansky

Bruce Lansky

Little Bad Wolf and Red Riding Hood

BY TIMOTHY TOCHER

No one had seen Big Bad Wolf for a week since the morning he'd gone hunting along the new road through the forest.

"Son," he'd said to Little Bad Wolf, "this road is just what we need. People always have plenty of food, and now they'll be bringing it right into the forest. Why, tricking them out of food is easier than catching a three-legged rabbit. I'll be back tonight with enough food to last us a week!"

But he hadn't come back.

Mother Wolf had been against the plan from the

start. She had many relatives who'd lost their lives dealing with people. Now, with winter approaching, she and Little Bad Wolf were alone and hungry.

"L. B., I'm not letting you leave this den until you promise to stay away from the road," Mother Wolf said. "No matter what your father says, you can't trust strangers."

L. B. promised, but he had no intention of keeping his word. He sneaked away and crouched in the bushes alongside the road, ready to jump out and threaten anyone who came along. One look at his snarling fangs, and any traveler who knew anything about his father would surely part with that information.

At last he heard gravel crunching. He hunkered down in the bushes and practiced making fierce faces. As the footsteps drew nearer, he prepared to pounce. Then he heard a strange sound. The walker was sighing.

L. B. peeked through the bushes and saw a tiny figure dressed all in red, carrying a basket so huge and heavy that it nearly dragged on the ground.

As the little girl passed his hiding place, L. B. noticed a red hood hanging down her back. "What a weird outfit," he thought.

Suddenly the girl stopped. To his surprise, she said,

"I feel someone watching me! Come out, whoever you are, and help me carry this basket. There's so much food in it that I can barely lift it."

"Food!" thought L. B. "Dad was right!"

Licking his chops, L. B. stepped out of the bushes behind the girl. "Did you say your basket is too heavy, little girl?" he asked.

The little girl reached into her hood and pulled out a spray can. She wheeled around and pointed it at L. B.'s drooling muzzle. "Freeze, Buster!" she cried. "One move and you're history!"

L. B. froze until he read the label on the can. Then his long snout stretched into a wolfy grin. "Oh please, little girl, don't squirt me with cheese spread! I'll have to spend all morning licking it off my fur."

The little girl lowered the can in disgust. "Well, it was either that or bop you over the head with a pepperoni. I'm too young to carry weapons."

"You don't need weapons with me. What's your name?"

"Everyone calls me Red Riding Hood, so you might as well, too. My mother got a deal on a bolt of red cloth, and she makes all my clothes from it. I talked her into adding this hood, hoping that she'll use up the material before I'm thirty."

"It's a nice color," said L. B., "but not for sneaking through the woods."

"Well, I've told you my name. Now what's yours? Or are you going to be as mysterious as the last wolf I met?"

"You met another wolf on this road?"

"Yup, about a week ago. I trudge this way every day—although my load was much lighter then. You still haven't told me your name."

"I'm L. B. Tell me: was this other wolf bigger than me?"

"Much bigger, L. B. He was a grownup, and you're still a pup, right?"

"A young adult, Red. Where did this other wolf go after you saw him?"

"I have no idea. He asked me a hundred questions, then took off without saying good-bye."

"That sounds like my dad. He's been missing for a week. Did you ask him to help you?"

"I sure did."

"And did he help?"

"No way! He said, 'We've all got problems, Kid,' and disappeared into the forest."

"That had to be my father. Where are you taking all this food, anyway?"

"Ha! That's the last thing your dad asked before he disappeared. Are you at least going to say good-bye if I answer?"

"I promise I'll do all I can to help you if you'll tell me what you told my dad," said L. B.

"I told him that my poor, dear old granny was sick and that I was bringing her a basket of food from my mom. Then he asked where she lived. I showed him the map Mom drew, and zip! he was gone!"

"And Granny's still sick?"

"It's very strange. I bring her a basket each day, and she moans and groans like she's dying. But then she gives me a list of food to bring, and it's always enough to feed an army. I don't know how an old lady who lies in bed all day can work up such an appetite. She eats like a—"

"Hold that thought, Red. Maybe I can help you out. Why don't you bring your basket this far each day, and I'll take it the rest of the way?"

"You would do that? But why?"

"I like you, Red. Not every kid would be so nice to an old lady. It shows you've got character."

"Thanks, L. B. You're sure different from your father. But there's one more part to the job. Granny always gives me a list for the next day. Would you bring that back here?"

"Sure. I'll leave the list right under that big rock by the roadside."

"You're the best, L. B.! I wish my mother could meet you. She always says, 'Don't talk to strangers, dear. Stay away from strangers, dear.'"

"My mom's the same way! I had to promise to stay away from the road before I could even leave the den this morning."

"Old people! Just because their generation can't be trusted, they want us to be suspicious of everyone. How can I repay you for helping me?"

"When Granny gets better, maybe you could bring a snack now and then for my poor mother and me. She's getting a little old to run down rabbits, and I haven't quite gotten the hang of this hunting business yet. Dad was giving me lessons when he disappeared."

"Poor L. B.! I've never had a father, so I know how you feel. It's a deal. Let's shake on it."

Red stuck out her tiny hand, and L. B. shook it with his hairy paw.

"Just one more thing, Red. Are there other houses on Granny's street?"

"Sure. Why?"

"Well, some folks act funny when they see a wolf in the neighborhood. How about lending me that red cloak so I can disguise myself when I leave the forest?"

"It's yours, L. B. I've got a closet full of them," sighed Red. She removed her cloak to reveal a red T-shirt and red pants. "Don't ask, L. B. The garments you can't see are red, too. I hate fabric sales!"

Happy to be free of her load, Red jogged off toward home. L. B. grunted as he picked up the basket. No wonder Red was dragging it! He had to see for himself the old lady who could eat this much in one day.

If only there were some way to lighten the basket. "Aha!" he thought and sat down in the shade of a roadside tree. He began to help himself to the goodies while he studied Red's map.

When his stomach was full, L. B. grabbed the still-heavy basket and started toward Granny's. At the edge of town, he donned the cloak, pulled on the hood, and headed down the street.

He wasn't used to being around so many people, and he was sure that his disguise wouldn't stand a close inspection. But no one seemed the least bit interested in him. People scurried this way and that, barely looking at each other.

At last he saw Granny's house. He walked up the driveway and knocked timidly on the door.

"Is that you, Red Riding Hood?" called a strangely familiar voice.

"Yes, Grandmother," L. B. rasped in his first-ever attempt at talking like a little girl.

"The door's unlocked. Come on in."

L. B. pushed and pulled at the door until he figured out how to turn the knob. Then he took a deep breath and went inside.

"Come back to my room, dear, and bring the basket. I'm too sick to get up."

Even though the day was sunny, Granny's bedroom was quite dark. She'd pulled all the shades. As L. B.'s eyes got used to the darkness, he could see the old lady lying in bed. The covers were pulled up almost to her eyes. On her head she wore a nightcap.

"Just leave the basket by the bed, dear, then feel free to run along. I don't want you wasting your whole day on an old lady like me."

"But how are you feeling, Granny?" asked L. B.

"About the same, dear. I hope you're not catching something yourself. Your voice sounds different today."

"Just a little cold, Granny—nothing to worry about. Let me feel your nose to see if it's dry."

Granny giggled. "That's how you tell if an animal's sick! People are sick when their foreheads are hot."

"Oh yeah . . . that's what I meant. Anyway, let me feel."

"No, no, dear. I took my temperature just before you arrived, and it was perfectly normal."

"I've forgotten, Granny—what is normal?"

"Oh, you know: not too hot, not too cold."

"Let me look in your eyes, then, to see if they're clear."

"I'm fine, Red, really. Now just take my list from the table by the door, and I'll see you tomorrow."

L. B. turned as if to leave and pretended to drop the list on the floor. As soon as he was below Granny's line of sight, he scooted to the foot of the bed. Reaching up, he groped under the covers until he found a pawful of bushy hair. Then he pulled it.

Out of the bed with a howl shot—not Granny—but his missing dad, Big Bad Wolf! He snarled at L. B., who calmly pulled off his hood and said, "Hi, Pop."

"Why, you little rascal! What did you do with Red?"

"Sent her home. I'm her new delivery boy. Where's Granny? Did you . . .?"

"No, no! Those old people are all skin and bones. They're not worth eating. She was gone when I got here. She'd tacked this note to the door."

Big Bad Wolf reached under the pillow and pulled out a sheet of paper bordered with fuzzy bunnies. He handed it to L. B., who read:

Dear Granddaughter,

Thank you for bringing me soup, but as you can see I'm not here to eat it. By the time you read this, I'll be in an airplane. My doctor says the only way I'll feel better is if I soak up some rays, so I'm off to Florida. Tell your mom I'll see her in the spring!

Love,
Granny

"Doesn't *anybody* stay with family anymore?" asked L. B.

"What's that supposed to mean?"

"Mom's been worried sick, Pop. All she can think about is her brother who had so much trouble with that boy, Peter. And her uncle who lost his life on that pig farm. And you've been lying here stuffing your face!"

"You've got me all wrong, son. Granny's got a huge freezer in the basement. I've been packing food into it all week."

"What good is that, Pop? We can't carry the freezer out of here, and sooner or later Red is bound to catch on."

"I worry about that kid. She's been here six times and still thinks I'm her granny. She must be as dumb as a rock. But come downstairs with me, L. B., and see what your old dad's been doing."

Big Bad Wolf led L. B. downstairs and opened Granny's giant freezer. L. B. began to salivate. The freezer was crammed with roasts, sandwiches, stews, pizzas, cakes, and pies.

"Let's eat, Pop! Then we'll bring some food back to Mom."

"Come here, boy."

Big Bad Wolf squeezed behind the freezer and

motioned for L. B. to follow. They stood peering into a hole in the earthen floor.

"I've started a tunnel leading to the woods. Once it's finished, we can go in and out all winter, grabbing food whenever we're hungry."

"How far have you gotten, Dad?"

"Not far. The ground is as hard as a hunter's heart. But together, I'm sure we'll make better progress."

Suddenly a blinding light filled the basement. Before the wolves could react, a bullhorn shrieked, "Come out from behind the freezer with your hands ... er ... paws up!"

The two wolves walked forward on their hind legs, with their front paws raised and shielding their eyes.

"Lie down on the floor and don't move!" boomed the voice. The shocked wolves obeyed.

Mercifully, the light went out. Then Red's voice said, "That's them, officers: the two rats—I mean wolves—who tricked me."

L. B. tried to smooth things over.

"Hi, Red! I found your missing food. My Pop and I are hiding down here to catch the crooks who are bothering Granny."

"Save your breath, Furball, and read this."

Red flicked a postcard across the room. It landed on the floor in front of the wolves' snouts. They read:

Dear Red,

The weather is here; wish you were beautiful! (Just kidding!) I miss you, but this Florida sunshine is doing the trick. Your old granny feels like a kid again.

Not all my friends are so lucky, Red. I'm worried about my next-door neighbors. They're stuck at home all winter, so I need a big favor. Could you and your mom bring them a daily basket? It would put my mind at ease.

Wait till you see the great bathing suit I'm bringing back for you. It's bright red, your favorite color!

Love,
Granny

L. B. started to speak, but a harsh voice interrupted. "Anything you say can and will be used against you in a court of law."

L. B. kept his snout to the ground, but raised his eyes. Two blue uniforms with shiny shoes, badges, and pistols towered over him and his dad. One officer was holding an enormous flashlight.

"Well, miss, we've got the big one on a ten-forty-three: impersonating a septuagenarian," said the officer with the flashlight.

The other whispered in Red's ear, "That means dressing like your granny."

"And a six-eighteen: unlawful entry with intent to commit a felony," continued the first officer.

"He broke into the house," translated the second.

"And conspiracy to deceive, a seven-four-niner!"

"He tried to trick you," explained the second officer.

"As for the little guy—" began the first officer.

"Stop!" shouted Red. "All I want to know is: what happens now?"

"Well," said the second officer, "it's reform school for the small one and prison for the big one. Wolves are pretty crafty, but they can't get out of this."

"And what happens to all the food in Granny's freezer?" Red asked.

"It's impounded as evidence!" thundered the first officer.

"That means—" began the second.

"That means it goes to waste," said Red, "and the

old couple next door goes hungry, unless my mother spends the whole winter cooking and I spend it dragging baskets through the woods. I've got a better idea."

"The law is the law," insisted the first officer. Red hoped the second officer might listen to reason.

"What if they admit they're guilty? Could they get off with community service?"

"No way!" shouted the first officer. "I caught them red-pawed. They're going to jail!"

"What's your idea, Red?" asked the second officer.

"Why can't they pay their debt to society by distributing all this food to people? These two can make sure no one in the neighborhood goes hungry."

"Oh, great. We'll be errand boys!" snarled Big Bad Wolf. But both he and L. B. knew this would be better than going to jail.

"It's your choice, lady," the first officer finally said. "But if these two miss one delivery, they're mine!"

"Don't worry, officer. I'll give the neighbors my phone number. One complaint, and you can have these crooks."

"Then we'll also have them on a three-two-five: failure to satisfy a verbal agreement. I like it!"

At last Big Bad Wolf and L. B. were allowed to go

back to the woods, their tails between their legs. They weren't looking forward to explaining their new obligation to Mother Wolf.

The police officers asked Red if she needed a ride home.

"Thanks, officers, but I'm in no hurry. My mother is going to find me guilty of a one-two-thousand."

"Gee, even I don't know that one!" admitted the first officer.

"She told me once; she told me twice; she told me a thousand times not to talk to strangers!" sighed Red.

And So They Did

BY V. McQuin

Once upon a time a queen had triplets.

"THREE! THREE?" the king shouted.

"Three! Three?" the servants cried.

"Three," the midwife said. And so there were.

"BOYS?" inquired the king.

"Boys?" asked the servants.

"Girls," said the midwife. And so they were. The queen named them April, May, and June.

As the years passed, the three little princesses grew into beautiful young women. One day the king said, "It is time for you to think of marrying."

"And wedding gowns, and wedding feasts, and wedding balls," said the servants.

"Not to mention princes," the queen said.

"Yes, princes," said the king, "and there is the problem. You see, there is a slight shortage of princes this year."

"A SHORTAGE OF PRINCES?" wailed the three princesses.

"How dreadful," said the servants.

"Most unfortunate," agreed the queen.

"I'm afraid so," said the king. "There were some very fine princes, but it appears they've all been taken. One was swept up by a cleaning girl."

"A CLEANING GIRL?" exclaimed the princesses.

"Impossible!" cried the servants.

"Of all the nerve," said the queen.

"A cleaning girl," said the king. "Named Cinder-something-or-other. Very nice and a hard worker, too. They say she had only rags to wear. Except for a pair of glass slippers. But she took the prince anyway."

The king continued, "Another prince found some enchanted castle. Those are rather rare these days, but you do find one every now and again. Seems everyone had been asleep for years, including the king's daughter, a real beauty. Without even knowing the girl, the prince fell in love. Woke her with a kiss."

"A KISS! A KISS?" gasped the three princesses.

"My word!" exclaimed the servants.

"Of course," said the queen.

"You know magic spells," the king said. "If you can't think of anything else to break them, a kiss will usually do the trick. Anyway, that prince was married before everyone could finish yawning.

"Another prince fell helplessly in love with a dead girl," the king went on.

"WITH A DEAD GIRL?" shouted the three princesses.

"How frightful," said the servants.

"Good heavens!" cried the queen.

"She wasn't really dead," the king said. "Another magic spell, you see. Her stepmother was a real witch. She couldn't stand the poor girl and put a curse on her. Everyone thought she was dead. She was so beautiful, they kept her in a glass coffin. Good thing, too. The prince wandered by and fell in love. A kiss did the trick again. One more prince taken. Lovely for them, but you see how it creates a problem for us."

"It's a problem, all right," said the princesses.

"And what a problem it is," said the servants.

"Most perplexing," the queen agreed.

Princess April stood up. "I will go and find a prince

myself," she said.

"FIND A PRINCE YOURSELF?" cried the king.

"Unheard of," scolded the servants.

"Quite improper," the queen agreed.

"I'm sure I can," said April. "If a cleaning girl can find a prince, how hard can it be?"

"Well . . . ," said the king, "I've heard a prince or two might be left in the northern countries. You could try there, I suppose."

"I will leave at once," said April. And so she did.

"What of you, May?" asked the king. "Will you seek out your prince, too?" asked the king.

"I hope you and Mother won't mind terribly, but I'd really rather not find a prince at all."

"NOT AT ALL?" shouted the king.

"Unthinkable," said the servants.

"Have you lost your mind?" asked the queen.

"Not at all," said Princess May. "I've never much liked being a princess. I'd prefer to be an ordinary sort of person and work in the gardens."

"Well . . . I suppose two princesses are enough for any castle," said the king.

"Indeed," said the servants.

"Of course," said the queen.

"And," said Princess May, "there's a nice young man who works in the gardens. I believe he would marry me if you said he could."

And so they did.

"Well then, June, what of you?" asked the king.

"Oh," said Princess June, "I think I'll put an ad in the paper."

"AN AD! IN THE PAPER?" cried the king, the queen, and the servants all at once.

"I'm quite happy being a princess," said Princess June, "but I don't want the hassle of searching for a prince. Therefore, I shall put an ad in the *Castle Times*. The ad will read:

> WANTED: A PRINCE TO MARRY
>
> PREFERABLY HANDSOME AND RICH
>
> MUST BE WISE AND KIND
>
> APPLY IN PERSON TO PRINCESS JUNE

"Well . . . ," said the king, "it's worth a try."

"Perhaps," said the servants.

"I'm not sure it's wise," said the queen.

"Sooner or later, a nice prince will answer my ad," said Princess June. "Until then, I'm quite content to wait."

"Very well," said the king. "Write your ad." And so she did.

It was not long before Princess April returned to the castle with a charming prince.

"Now then, April, tell us how you found this fellow," said the king.

"It wasn't easy, Father," Princess April answered. "I traveled north until I reached a castle. A queen and her son lived in it, but they wouldn't even talk about marriage. 'Spend the night and we'll talk in the morning,' the queen said. The room was nice enough, but oh, the bed! I needed a ladder to climb into it. And was it ever lumpy! I couldn't sleep a bit. I figured that since I was awake, and the prince didn't seem very eager to marry me, I might as well move on. So I did.

"Of course, it was terribly dark out. I couldn't see a thing. I ran right into the side of another castle. When I rang the bell, a horrid beast came to the door!"

"A BEAST! A HORRID BEAST?" cried the king.

"Shocking," said the servants.

"Extraordinary," said the queen.

"It was dreadful," said Princess April. "You can be sure I didn't stick around to find a prince there! I ran away as quickly as I could in the dark.

"Suddenly, I splashed right into a smelly pond. A poor frog talked to me. Or at least he tried. He had a raspy voice—hard to understand. I was tired, frightened, and soaked—I didn't have time to listen to a croaky old frog."

"That may have been a good time to try a kiss," said the king.

"Ah . . . yes, indeed," said the servants.

"Quite so," said the queen.

"A kiss! Hmm . . . ," said Princess April, "I never thought to kiss a *frog*. . . ."

"Not to worry, my dear. You've a prince now," comforted the queen. "Do tell us how you got him."

"Oh, yes. In the morning, I wandered farther north. The snow was very deep. I was freezing, not to mention tired and hungry. I almost decided to go home and let my prince find me. Then I saw him! He was so tall, so handsome, so marvelous that I almost didn't notice he was made of ice."

"OF ICE! HE WAS MADE OF ICE?" exclaimed the king.

"Remarkable," the servants said.

"Chilling!" said the queen.

"Indeed," agreed Princess April, and her prince

nodded and shivered. "He was enchanted, of course. By a wicked stepmother. You know how it is."

"And you thawed him out?" asked the king.

"A kiss did the trick, just as you said," Princess April answered. "As soon as he stopped dripping, we hurried here to be married."

"Everything is almost ready for the wedding," the queen said. "While you were away, we worked day and night to prepare your wedding feast, ball, and gowns."

"Gowns?" asked Princess April.

"May has arranged to marry a young man who works in the gardens," the king said.

"IN THE GARDENS! MAY IS MARRYING A GARDENER?" cried Princess April.

"It's true," said the servants.

"And why not?" said the queen.

"Of course," said the king, "he isn't just a gardener. He's a prince as well. Wicked stepfather, curses, and all that. A kiss did the trick once more. We can have a triple wedding as soon as a suitable prince answers June's ad."

"AD! JUNE HAS PLACED AN AD FOR A PRINCE?" Princess April cried.

"Most upsetting," said the servants.

"Quite distressing," agreed the queen.

"We've already been through this," said the king.

Just then, the bell rang. The servants shouted, "A prince!"

"Lower the drawbridge!" the king called.

Princess June opened the door. She saw no one. Just as she turned to go back inside, she heard a very small laugh.

"Hello?" the princess said, looking all around her.

"Ha! Tricked you, didn't I?" A very small man popped out of a crack between the paving stones. He was riding a mouse.

"Oh!" cried Princess June, backing away.

"Tom Thumb at your service," the little man said. "I'm here about the ad. May I speak to Princess June, please?"

"Why . . . I am Princess June, but I'm afraid you are not quite what I was hoping for. You're much too small, and . . . I . . . well, I'm afraid of mice. I'm sorry, but you just won't do."

"Oh well, it was worth a try. I guess I'll be off. Good day." Tom Thumb hopped into his saddle and spurred the mouse away.

"Well?" the king asked when she came inside.

Princess June shook her head. "It was a very odd little man, only as big as your thumb. His horse was a mouse! I doubt he's really a prince. Oh, there's the bell again. Perhaps this will be my prince."

The drawbridge was lowered again. Princess June opened the door—and slammed it shut.

"Well?" said the king.

"So?" said the servants.

"A kiss wouldn't help?" asked the queen.

"Absolutely not!" said June. "The ad must have gotten into the *Jungle Times* by mistake. It was a lion."

"A LION?" shouted the king.

"Beastly," said the servants.

"I knew the ad was a mistake," said the queen.

"Perhaps you're right," said Princess June, peeking out the door. "But the lion's gone now. And look, someone else is coming."

"A man, I hope," said the king.

"A tall and handsome man," said the servants.

"Please," prayed the queen.

Princess June opened the door. The man was indeed tall and handsome. But he was not a prince.

"I understand you are looking for a new gardener," he said.

"Actually," said Princess June, "I'm looking for a prince to marry me."

The man was not a prince, but he was charming, kind, and wise. "Well now, you are a very beautiful princess," he said. "I would be delighted to marry you. Although I am not a prince now, I would be if I married a princess. Marry me and you shall have your prince."

From behind the door, the king, queen, servants, and other princesses said, "TAKE HIM!" And so she did.

The next day, the castle was full of flowers and wedding guests. The three princesses were full of happiness; the king and queen were full of pride; the servants were full of relief.

It was a marvelous wedding. The three princesses were stunning in their wedding gowns of silk, lace, beads, and jewels. The three princes were dashing in their wedding suits. The feast was delicious. No one went hungry in all the land that day. The dance could not have been better, even though someone dropped a glass slipper. It was a glorious day.

As the newlyweds kissed, everyone was certain the three princesses and their princes would live happily ever after.

And so they did.

King Midas

BY TIMOTHY TOCHER

Once upon a dime, about a quarter century ago, there lived a banker named King Midas. King had a loving wife and son, but he barely noticed them. He spent every waking hour at the bank so he could be near his money.

King was born to be a banker. He talked toddlers into smashing their piggy banks and opening accounts. He convinced senior citizens to empty their cookie jars and trust him with their savings.

Saturday was King's favorite day of the week. The bank was closed so there were no customers or tellers milling about. King claimed it gave him a chance to catch up on his paperwork, but in truth, he just wanted to be alone with his money.

This particular Saturday was a scorcher. King sat in the still bank, jacket off and shirtsleeves rolled up. He had removed his shoes and socks and had buried each bare foot in a bucket of cool coins. As he added columns of figures, King wiggled his toes in ecstasy.

A tapping on the bank's front door drew King's attention.

"We're closed!" King shouted.

The tapping went on. King tried to ignore it, but he couldn't concentrate. Besides, it was almost time for him to enter the vault and bury himself in greenbacks. He wanted no interruptions then. Sighing, he pulled his feet out of the buckets and began putting on his shoes and socks.

At last he opened the bank door. A small man in a black suit stood holding his hat in his hands.

"We're closed Saturdays," King snapped. "Come back Monday after nine."

As King started to close the door, the stranger reached into his jacket pocket and pulled out an enormous roll of large bills.

"Ben Franklin and U. S. Grant!" King was suddenly all smiles. "My two favorite Americans! Won't you come in, Mr. . . . ?"

"Conscience," the man said.

"Catchy name. Can't say I've heard it before. I'm King Midas, the president of this fine financial institution. No deposit is too small or too large for my personal attention."

"Are you convertible, Mr. Midas?" the stranger asked softly.

"Convertible? I can convert that cash into stocks, bonds, real estate, or whatever you'd care to invest in. Step into my office."

"I don't want to convert my money, Mr. Midas. I'm here to convert you," Conscience said as he and King sat down on opposite sides of King's desk.

"I'm not sure what you mean, Mr. Conscience, but if Franklin and Grant want to convert me, I'm happy to oblige."

"Do you know where your son is today, Mr. Midas?"

"Prince? He's home with his mom. Why?"

"How old is your son, Mr. Midas?"

"Um, let's see. He's seven . . . no, eight! Eight years old."

"He's twelve, Mr. Midas, and today he's pitching the championship game for his Little League team. The field is just down the block. Why don't you take some time off and watch him?"

"Take time off? Who's going to do my paperwork if I'm sitting at a ball game? And how do you know so much about my son, anyway?"

"Everyone in town knows Prince is a fine pitcher. I suggest you share some time with him before it's too late. Your boy is growing up without you. You can do your paperwork next week."

"Now look, Mr. Conscience, I don't need your advice. Are you interested in depositing your money or not?"

"Is money all you think about? Your son needs you."

"He needs my money, Conscience," King was getting annoyed and so began to forgo formalities. "When I was his age I didn't even have decent clothes to wear—never mind a baseball uniform. It's because I work so hard that he's out there playing ball."

"But now you have enough money. Go to the game."

"I could never have enough money, Conscience. It takes hard work to make money, more work to keep it, and even more to make it grow. Do you think I just stick out my hand and money appears in it?"

"Suppose it were that simple. What if everything you touched turned to money? Would that make you happy?"

"You bet!"

"Then you've got it, Midas. From now on whatever you touch will turn to money."

Conscience vanished. King's mouth dropped open. He looked under his desk—nothing but buckets of coins.

He blinked and shook his head. "Maybe I *am* working too hard. I think I'll relax in my nice, cool vault."

As King pushed back his chair, its arms turned from brown to green. Looking closer, he realized the chair was now made of tightly rolled dollar bills. His heart leapt.

King reached out and touched some items on his desk. A pen, a calculator, and a calendar instantly changed into bills and coins.

"Yippee!" King yelled. He threw a handful of paper clips in the air and enjoyed the shower of quarters bouncing off his head and shoulders.

King looked at the floor. It seemed normal despite the fact that his feet were touching it. Apparently only his hands possessed the magic touch.

Midas was dying to show off his new power. "The ball game! Wait until my wife sees this! We're rich!"

He darted toward the front door and grabbed the

knob. To his delight, it became a shiny silver dollar. Unfortunately, the dollar fell to the floor and rolled away. Without a handle, King couldn't open the door.

King headed for the fire exit at the rear of the building. He pushed it open with his backside. An alarm bell started to clang. He ducked outside and bumped the door shut with his hip. Then he scooted off toward the ballpark.

Along the way, King delighted in his new power. He touched everything he could: tree branches, flowers, and crumpled paper that littered the sidewalk. Although he scooped up the first pile of coins and rolls of dollar bills that fell from his fingers, soon his excitement overcame him. He ran faster and faster, leaving the money on the ground to be picked up by incredulous pedestrians.

When King arrived at the field, the score was tied. Prince fired a third strike past a burly batter. Prince and his teammates raced off the field for their turn at bat.

"King, is it really you?"

He looked up to see his wife leaning out of the bleachers. Smiling and waving, he walked over to join her. But when his hand brushed the bleachers, the entire structure turned into dollar bills and collapsed.

Stunned fans landed in a heap on the ground. They soon forgot their scrapes and bruises and began grappling furiously with each other over the money

Mrs. Midas made her way though the crowd and stared at her husband. "What is going on? I knew you wouldn't come here if everything were all right. You haven't come to a game in years!"

"I don't understand it myself, honey. This crazy customer at the bank cast a spell on me. It's great! Everything I touch turns to money. We'll be the richest people in the world!"

"So you think it's great, do you? How about Prince?"

Midas looked toward the field. The umpire was busily brushing off home plate. Prince knelt alone in the on-deck circle, holding a bat. Everyone else, coaches and players, had joined the scramble for money.

"What a chump!" Midas said. "All that cash flying around, and he doesn't even go for his share."

"He's not the chump in this family," retorted Mrs. Midas. "Five minutes ago these boys were playing baseball, working together for a common goal. Now they're at each other's throats over a few dollars." Midas could see players wrestling on the ground.

"At least go say hello to him," Mrs. Midas urged.

King trudged over to the on-deck circle. "Hi, Prince. Sorry about the game. Looks as though you may have to finish it some other day."

"Dad! You came to see me?"

"Don't act so shocked. I've seen you play before."

"Yeah, but that was tee-ball. I was only eight then."

"Well, I'm here now. How come you're moping around by yourself?"

"Do you see how those people are fighting for that money, Dad?"

"I sure do," King chuckled.

"I was thinking: if we had a raffle at each game, we could draw twice as many fans and raise some money for the Little League."

"That's a good idea, son."

"And all those extra people would spend money at the concession stand. You just watch: those people who are fighting for money will walk over and spend it on hot dogs, sodas, and popcorn. The concession-stand owner will end up with the money without fighting anyone."

"You're thinking like a real businessman, son. I didn't know you had it in you."

"I love playing baseball, Dad. But that's not all I

think about. How about we buy that concession stand before next season? I think we could turn it into a real moneymaker."

"Hey, now you're talking, son. It's a deal. Let's shake on it."

"TIME!" yelled the umpire, throwing his arms in the air. His voice froze King and Prince, their hands inches apart. He strode over and placed himself between father and son.

"Is it SAFE! to shake his hand? What happens when your fingers STRIKE! his? Are you OUT! of your mind?" cried the umpire.

King remembered his magic touch. "I forgot. But how did you—?" The umpire raised his mask. "Conscience! What are you doing here?"

"I'm giving you a chance to reconsider, Mr. Midas. Do you still think your magic touch is a gift? You'll never be able to touch your wife or son again."

King thought of how exciting it was to create instant money. Then he imagined what it would be like to share his business knowledge with Prince, to pass on what he had learned. Prince was peeking around Conscience now, wondering what was going on. King had a fleeting vision of his son turned into a dollar bill, blowing away across the baseball field. He shuddered. No amount of money could replace his son.

"I return your gift, Mr. Conscience, and I thank you for the opportunity."

Conscience smiled and said, "Good choice, King. As of this second, you no longer have the power. And everything is now as it was." Then he pulled down his mask and bellowed, "PLAY BALL!"

Fans gawked as the money in their hands suddenly disappeared and the bleachers materialized out of thin air. Then, after they rubbed their eyes and shook their heads, they began to climb back to their seats. Players and coaches suddenly remembered the game and hustled back to their positions.

Prince gripped his father's hand firmly, smiled, and headed for the on-deck circle. King joined his wife in the bleachers, put his arm around her shoulders, and watched proudly as Prince warmed up.

But old habits die hard. During the game, King silently counted the fans and estimated how much each person spent on food during an average game.

"Does Prince ever play doubleheaders?" he asked.

Jill and the Beanstalk

BY DENISE VEGA

Many years ago, in a cottage in a valley, a poor widow lived with her daughter, Jill. One harsh winter, Jill's mother took ill. Jill had to stay home and care for her mother, so she couldn't go and find work. When Jill couldn't squeeze even one more drop of milk out of their cow, Buttercup, Jill and her mother both knew the cow would have to go.

"I'll get a good price for her, Mother," said Jill. She waved good-bye and led Buttercup along the path toward the marketplace.

When they arrived, the plaza was teeming with vil-

39

lagers and noisy vendors.

"Vegetables for sale! Fresh vegetables!"

"Cotton! Clean cotton here!"

Jill dragged Buttercup from booth to booth, looking for a buyer. But no one was interested in the scrawny, milkless cow. Discouraged, Jill slumped down on the town-hall steps.

"Fine cow, miss," said a gruff voice. Jill looked up, startled, and saw an old man with a long, snowy beard.

"She has stopped giving milk," Jill said. "You can have her for two shillings."

"I have no money," said the old man.

Jill sighed. "When it comes to this cow, no one does."

"But I do have these," he said, thrusting his wrinkled hand in her face. He opened his fingers slowly to reveal their contents.

"You expect me to trade a cow for a bunch of beans? You're crazy." Jill stood up and grasped Buttercup's rope. "I guess I'll have to sell you to the butcher, Buttercup. Mother and I need money to buy food."

"Wait." The old man grabbed her sleeve. "These are magic beans. If you plant them tonight, they will grow into a giant beanstalk by morning. Climb to the top of the beanstalk and enter the castle in the clouds. There you'll find all the gold you'll ever need."

"If those beans are so great, why don't you plant them yourself?" Jill asked suspiciously.

"Alas," said the man, pulling a decaying piece of parchment from his coat, "I cannot. The finder of the beans cannot use them. However, if I trade the beans in an honest exchange, I will receive a golden egg once a year for twenty years."

Jill read the parchment carefully. It seemed legitimate. But how could she risk her only source of income on the words of this strange old man?

"Tell you what," she said, pulling a piece of fresh parchment from her own pocket. "I'll give your beans a try with the condition that, if they don't work, Buttercup is mine again."

She scribbled several lines on the parchment. "You may sleep in our barn tonight, and we will determine our fates tomorrow." She smoothed the parchment on the top step. "Sign and date here, here, and here."

Jill's mother was surprised when she saw her daughter return with the cow and a stranger, but when Jill explained her plan, the widow agreed to try it.

"But I want you to tie Buttercup to the front rail," she said, "so we can hear if the old man tries to steal her away in the night."

After supper, Jill dug a shallow hole and dropped the beans inside. She covered them with soil and watered them generously.

"Okay," she said to the old man, brushing the dirt from her hands, "let's see if you are worthy of my trust." The three of them said good-night and went to bed.

The next morning, Jill awoke in darkness. "It can't still be nighttime," she thought. She went to the window, pulled the curtains aside, . . . and gasped.

A thick, green, twisting vine was growing outside her window, its leaves as large as the seat of a chair. Jill called to her mother as she tugged on her clothes.

The old man was standing at the foot of the beanstalk, rubbing his hands with glee. "See? See, young miss? I told you the beans would sprout."

Jill nodded, but didn't smile. "Your story about the beanstalk is true, but I have yet to see any gold," she said, placing her foot on one of the bottom leaves. "Your word is not good with me yet."

Hand over hand, foot over foot, Jill climbed the mighty stalk, which vanished into the clouds thousands of feet in the air. When she popped through the top of the clouds, Jill saw a road stretching out before her. It led to a magnificent castle.

Jill caught her breath and headed down the road. When she reached the castle, she knocked hard on the huge oak door. She soon heard booming footsteps, then the door swung open, and Jill looked straight into a huge white curtain. A moment later, she realized she was standing in front of a very large woman, and that the curtain was actually the woman's apron.

"Yes?" A thunderous voice from above nearly knocked Jill off her feet.

"Excuse me, ma'am," Jill said, waving her arms and jumping up and down.

"Oh, there you are," said the woman, bending over to squint into Jill's face.

"Hello, my name's Jill. I wonder if you have any gold to which I'm entitled."

The woman scratched her chin, then rubbed her head. "Not that I know of." She paused. "My husband has a wonderful gold harp and a hen that lays golden eggs, but I don't think he'd give either of those up. In fact, when one boy tried to steal them, my husband put a stop to it pretty quickly."

Jill groaned. "The old man didn't say anything about giants," she muttered as she peered around the woman's skirt and saw the oversized hats hanging on hooks by the door and an array of swords in a stand nearby.

The woman leaned down again. "Why don't you come in for a cup of tea? My husband's out, and I'd surely love some company."

Jill followed the woman inside, marveling at the beautiful castle. "It's so lovely up here, I would think you'd have lots of visitors," Jill said as the woman picked her up and set her on the table.

"Oh, we don't want for visitors. Children often find their way here. My husband likes them a lot. Perhaps too much." She poured herself a cup of tea and poured some for Jill into a thimble.

"So why are you lonely? Don't they ever come back to see you again?" Jill sipped her tea and nibbled the bread placed before her.

"No, my husband eats them," sighed the woman. She shook her head as though it were just a bad habit, like picking his nose or chewing with his mouth open.

"Eats them?" Jill cried, leaping to her feet. She scurried to the edge of the table and looked over the edge. It was quite high, but she thought she could make it.

"No need for you to worry, miss," said the woman, gently tugging her back. "He doesn't like girls. Just little boys. It's a taste thing."

"A taste thing," Jill repeated. Her heart still thumped with panic. Then she sat up. "Girls don't taste as good as boys?" she asked indignantly.

"Guess not," said the woman. "Too many brains, he says. Brains taste nasty, and the nerves get stuck between his teeth."

Jill nodded. She had just bitten into her bread when the table began to tremble.

Thud! The front door slammed against the wall.

"Oh, he's home!" shouted the woman happily. "He'll be thrilled that we have company. In here, honey!"

Thump! Thump! Thump!

"Fee, fi, fo, fum, I smell the blood of . . . an Englishwoman." A giant man burst into the kitchen and stared in disappointment at Jill. "What a letdown," he said, leaning his sword in the corner. He came over to the table and sniffed her head.

"Hey!" Jill said, brushing him away.

"I so wanted another boy," he lamented, slumping into his chair. "They're very tasty." He studied her as though he were imagining how she might taste roasted with a bit of onion and celery and just a dash of pepper.

"I'm very smart. Lots of brains," Jill said, tapping

her head as she edged backward across the table.

The giant grimaced. "Brains? Yuck." He spat on the floor as his wife set a steaming bowl of stew in front of him. "Well, it's nice to have the company, anyway." He began slurping his stew hungrily.

As he ate, Jill's fears subsided a bit. She told the giants about the magic beans and the old man's promise of riches.

"I don't give anything away," said the giant. "But maybe we can work something out." He turned to his wife. "Honey, if you're finished with your meal, would you mind bringing in Goldie?"

"Not at all, Poopsie." The woman disappeared and returned with a large brown hen. She placed the hen in a basket on the floor next to the table.

"Okay, Goldie, lay one on me," said the giant. The hen settled in, gave a few cackles and squawks, and stepped out of the basket.

"Whoa!" exclaimed Jill. "That's some egg!"

The giant leaned down, picked up the egg between his thumb and forefinger, and set it before Jill. She shook her head in disbelief, envisioning the food she could buy and the fences she could mend with just one such golden egg. She reached out for it.

"Ah, ah, ah. No touching." The giant plucked it away before Jill's fingers even brushed its shining shell.

"She lays one whenever you ask?" Jill asked.

The giant nodded.

"And they're always solid gold?"

"Yep."

Jill scratched her chin, then rubbed her head. "Okay, so what can I do to earn one of these things?"

Now the giant scratched his chin. A sparrow popped out of his beard and perched on his shoulder. "I don't think we have any work for you," he said. "What there is to do, my wife and I do ourselves."

Jill thought for a moment. "Is there anything you want that I can get for you?"

The giant thought for a moment. "Well, there is one thing we're sadly lacking." He looked over at his wife, and she nodded.

"Friends," they said in unison.

Jill laughed. "Well, it's a bit difficult to make friends when you keep eating the prospects."

The giant nodded contritely. "I can't help it, though. The boys are so tasty."

"And the girls don't stay very long," said the woman, "when they learn what happens to the boys."

Jill rubbed her head again, then stood up and looked around. "Would you mind giving me a tour?"

"Not at all," the giant replied, holding out his hand. He hoisted her onto his unoccupied shoulder and carried her through a maze of rooms and hallways.

Jill marveled at the huge ballroom with its many chandeliers glittering like stars. The tower view was breathtaking—miles of clouds as far as the eye could see. And every chair, table, painting, and statue were humongous—just the right size for a pair of giants.

When the tour ended, Jill said, "I've got a plan."

And so Giant Castle Tours was born.

"You'll soon have a constant stream of visitors," Jill told the giants. "But you, sir, must promise not to eat the boys who come through. In exchange for meeting all these people, you will pay me one golden egg per month, as well as one golden egg per year for the old man who gave me the magic beans."

The giant bit his lip. "The egg part is fine. But couldn't I have one out of every ten boys?"

Jill shook her head.

"One out of a hundred?"

"Zero," Jill said, making a big O with her fingers and thumb.

The giant looked so dejected, Jill felt sorry for him. "Look, you just can't go around eating little boys. Their parents will be very upset, and you definitely won't have any friends."

"All right," the giant agreed with a heavy sigh.

"Here," Jill said, holding out a piece of parchment. "Write down everything that makes boys tasty, and I'll find a food that tastes just as good."

And so the deal was struck. Jill soon opened the Giant Castle Tours, guiding visitors through the castle and introducing people from around the country to the lonely giants. People lined up daily at the base of the magic beanstalk. The old man sold tickets, looking very distinguished with his long white beard and brass-buttoned uniform. He was glad to have something to do and a regular income. Buttercup, the cow, grazed in a field nearby, mooing happily at all the attention she received for being "the cow that started it all."

The people who took the tour spread the word that it was worth every penny and the long climb. They raved about everything, from the tower vista, to the harp concert the giant gave every afternoon. But best of all, they gushed, was Goldie, the hen, who sat on her nest in the center of the ballroom, surrounded by an amazing collection of golden eggs in glass cases.

With the eggs she received as payment and the money she made from the tours, Jill hired a doctor for her mother, repaired their cottage, and stocked their food cellar for years to come.

The giant couple so enjoyed their new friends, they climbed down the beanstalk once a week to visit the village. The villagers would ask them to perform small tasks, such as repairing damaged chimneys or rescuing cats from the church steeple, all the while laughing and talking. The giants became so popular that Jill hired a man to set up appointments for them.

Things couldn't have worked out better, except that every so often, Jill would catch the giant nibbling the elbow of an unsuspecting boy. His wife would pull him away while Jill rubbed salve on the frightened boy's skin and led him to another part of the castle.

Once a day, Jill brought the giant a plate of "boy substitute." The hard shells were nearly as crunchy as bones, and the hot, spicy tofu, lettuce, tomatoes, onions, and cheese resembled the innards of a freshly roasted boy.

The giant was definitely acquiring a taste for tacos.

The Prince and the Pea

BY BRUCE LANSKY

There once was a very serious young prince named Ferdinand. During his four years in college, Prince Ferdinand learned several languages and studied art, literature, and music as well as government and international relations. When he completed his studies, his parents asked him to come home and attend to his royal duties. They were hoping that he would start looking for a bride.

Now, some princes spend all their time having fun—jetting off to Rio for Mardi Gras, to the Alps for skiing, or to Monte Carlo for gambling. But not

Ferdinand.

He took his royal position seriously. Prince Ferdinand visited hospitals and brought toys to sick children. He raised money for worthy charities. And he hosted diplomatic events to help improve his country's relations with its neighbors. Prince Ferdinand wanted to be a worthy successor when his father, King Carlos, retired.

But when his mother, Queen Isabella, introduced him to young women from the royal courts of England, Norway, and Monaco, Prince Ferdinand was not particularly interested. Although the women were exquisitely dressed and quite beautiful, he found them boring. After a few minutes conversing about the weather, Prince Ferdinand would excuse himself and return to his reading or music. When his mother asked him what he thought of a young woman, he would often say, "She's not a true princess."

Queen Isabella would retort, "What are you talking about? She's from one of the finest families in Europe." But Prince Ferdinand would stick to his opinion.

The king and queen began to worry that Ferdinand would never marry and produce a royal heir. So they decided to do something about it.

"Ferdinand claims he's looking for a 'true princess,'" exclaimed Queen Isabella. "I know how we can find one—the old-fashioned way."

The following week the king and queen invited the fifty most eligible young women in all of Spain to a slumber party. While the daughters of dukes, earls, and barons buzzed excitedly about the event, the queen prepared the palace. Fifty bed frames were carried into the royal ballroom. On each bed frame was a mattress filled with the finest goose down. On each mattress were sheets of the finest silk. On top of the sheets was a blanket made of the softest lamb's wool. And at the head of each bed was a goose-down pillow in a silk pillowcase.

Queen Isabella supervised the chambermaids as they made each bed. If the sheets were not tucked in properly, the queen ordered the bed remade. After the chambermaids had finished and left the ballroom, the queen put an uncooked pea under each mattress.

That evening a sumptuous dinner was served. All the guests were seated at the royal table, with King Carlos and Queen Isabella at one end and Prince Ferdinand at the other.

Queen Isabella addressed the excited young

women: "We've invited you to spend this evening with us for a special reason. Prince Ferdinand would like to marry a 'true princess.' Perhaps one of you is that special someone. Tomorrow morning he will interview each of you."

The young women could hardly wait for morning. When dinner was over, they all retired directly to their beds. Meanwhile, Prince Ferdinand paced his room. How could he possibly pick a true princess on the basis on one brief meeting?

The next morning, King Carlos, Queen Isabella, and Prince Ferdinand gathered in the royal dining room. They sat on one side of the table; an empty chair was on the other side. Every five minutes, the royal butler escorted a young woman to the table. She was introduced and seated in the empty chair. Then the queen would ask one question: "How did you sleep?"

The first young woman said, "I couldn't sleep a wink. The lumpy pillow kept me up all night." "She's not a true princess," said Queen Isabella. "Next!" said the king.

The second young woman said, "The blanket was too hot. Then, when I took it off, the air conditioning was too cool." "She's not a true princess," said Queen

Isabella. "Next!" said the king.

One by one the young women moaned about sleepless nights. One was bothered by the snoring young woman next to her. Another was allergic to silk. Another had left her sleeping mask at home. The list of complaints was endless. After each young woman aired her complaint, Queen Isabella declared that she wasn't a true princess, and the king signaled the butler to escort the young woman out.

The fiftieth young woman was different. She didn't just complain about the air conditioning or the blankets or the pillow—she complained about everything, including a lumpy mattress.

"What did you say?" asked Queen Isabella.

"I said, '. . . and to add insult to injury, there was a lump in my mattress,'" snapped the young woman.

"We've finally found a true princess!" announced the queen.

Prince Ferdinand nervously said, "I'm sorry, Mother, but I don't share your opinion," and bolted out of the room. The idea of marrying any of those fifty unpleasant young women filled him with dread. He quickly changed into blue jeans and a T-shirt so he could go for a horseback ride without attracting any attention.

Striding into the royal stables, Prince Ferdinand noticed a young woman sleeping in the hayloft. As he approached his favorite horse, Diego, the horse whinnied, waking her. She opened her eyes, stretched, and began brushing the hay from her hair and clothes.

"I'm sorry we woke you up," Prince Ferdinand apologized. Not recognizing her, he added, "but why were you sleeping in the stable?"

Assuming she was speaking to a groom, the young woman blurted out her story. "I was invited to the royal slumber party. But when the queen announced that Prince Ferdinand would interview all the guests the next morning for the purpose of choosing a bride, I left. I have no interest in marrying someone who would choose his wife in such a ridiculous manner," she explained.

"Neither would I," Prince Ferdinand agreed. "But fifty young women were invited, and fifty guests were in the grand ballroom," he puzzled.

"How do you know?" asked the young woman.

Realizing that the young woman did not recognize him, Prince Ferdinand said, "One of the cooks told me."

"Well," she went on, "I exchanged clothes with Conchita, a very rude chambermaid. Then I took a coffee cup from the dinner table and put it under her mattress to make sure she would get no sleep at all. I stuck around so I could find out whom the prince selects as the 'true princess.'"

The prince couldn't help laughing, even though her practical joke was on him.

"By the way, have you heard whether the prince has made up his mind yet?" the young woman asked.

"I doubt that he'll live happily ever after with the charming Conchita," Prince Ferdinand responded. This time it was the young woman who laughed.

Prince Ferdinand studied the young woman. She was dressed in ill-fitting servant's clothes and was rumpled from sleeping in the stable, but the mischievous sparkle in her eyes captivated him.

"I admire your wit and your courage," he said. "What a wonderful joke to play on the prince. While we're waiting to find out what he decides, perhaps you'd like to wash and put on some clean clothes."

Prince Ferdinand led the young woman to the bathhouse near the royal swimming pool, where she showered and changed into Ferdinand's sweatshirt and jeans, which were several sizes too big. The prince and his friend then snuck into the palace through the kitchen door. "Would you mind waiting here while I find some breakfast for you?" he asked.

"Not at all," she responded.

Prince Ferdinand left his friend in the kitchen and returned to the dining room, where the king and queen were still interviewing Conchita. Between yawns, Conchita was grumpily adding to her list of complaints. Ferdinand could see that his mother's initial excitement at discovering a true princess had turned to horror at the prospect of having such an unpleasant young woman in the family.

"Mother and Father," Ferdinand said. "I think you should see for yourself why Conchita thought that her mattress was lumpy." Conchita led the royal family to her bed, and the prince lifted the mattress. Sure enough, underneath the mattress was a royal coffee cup.

"Conchita's not a true princess," Ferdinand whispered, and the queen breathed a deep sigh of relief. She signaled the butler to usher Conchita out of the palace.

"I'd like to introduce you to our fiftieth guest, but I'm sorry to say I don't know her name yet," said Prince Ferdinand to his parents. Then he opened the kitchen door and invited his new friend into the dining room.

The young woman's eyes opened wide when she saw the king and queen. At the same time, she realized that her new friend was none other than Prince Ferdinand.

Now that Conchita was gone, Queen Isabella's attention focused on the young woman dressed in Prince Ferdinand's sweatshirt and jeans. "She couldn't possibly be one of our guests," said the queen. "I've already interviewed fifty young women."

"Permit me to explain," interjected the young woman. "My name is Marisa de Santiago. You know my father, Don Domingo. You knighted him for building a library in our village. I was, indeed, one of your fifty guests. At dinner when you said the prince was looking for a 'true princess,' I realized that he might propose marriage. But I could never marry anyone unless I loved him. So I invited a rude chambermaid, Conchita, to take my place." The queen and king exchanged an embarrassed glance.

"Where did you sleep, my dear?" asked Queen Isabella.

"I slept in the royal stables."

"How did you sleep?" asked the queen.

"I slept quite royally," Marisa quipped.

Queen Isabella and King Carlos couldn't help smiling. They turned to Prince Ferdinand and noticed that he was smiling, too.

"Well," harrumphed King Carlos, "what do you have to say for yourself, young man?"

"Father," Ferdinand replied, "all I can say is that I am delighted to make Marisa's acquaintance, and I think I will enjoy getting to know her. I hope the feeling is mutual."

Marisa smiled in agreement.

Turning to Marisa, he said, "You must be starving. Would you care to join us for breakfast?"

"With pleasure," she smiled.

In time, the friendship between Prince Ferdinand and Marisa grew into love. About a year after the happy couple was married, they had a beautiful baby girl. Everyone, including Queen Isabella, agreed that she was a true princess.

The Real Story of Sleeping Beauty

BY LIYA LEV OERTEL

Sleeping Beauty's real name was Priscilla, and she was no beauty. Don't get me wrong: she was very pretty on the outside, but on the inside . . . that was a different story entirely. Her beautiful blond hair did fall in perfect curls, but she made five maids redo it a dozen times each morning, just to be mean. And while she did have big, blue eyes, they never twinkled with merriment. Instead, they glinted with malice and glared with anger. Her pretty mouth never smiled. It was too busy pouting, whining, and yelling.

Since the day she was born, Priscilla was absolutely

convinced that she was far superior to everybody, and she treated all her parents' subjects and servants accordingly. She ordered them about day and night, making them run back and forth for her pleasure.

She never said "please" or "thank you." Instead, she stamped her feet, shook her fists, and complained about everything. Nothing was ever good enough: her meals were too hot or too cold, her dresses were too tight or too loose, the furniture was too hard or too soft, and so on. As you can well imagine, not only did Priscilla dislike everybody, but the feeling was definitely mutual.

Priscilla's parents, the king and the queen, were very kind. They loved their subjects and ruled them fairly. They were both extremely distressed about their only child's behavior and did all they could to improve her disposition. When Priscilla was a child, they hired the best storytellers and musicians to perform for her. They brought in other children for Priscilla to play with and filled her room with piles of toys. But Priscilla was rude to the storytellers, broke the musicians' instruments, and chased away the children. She hoarded her toys and asked for more, but she never played with them.

The king and queen became desperate. They even tried putting extra sugar into her meals, hoping to sweeten her temper. But although the court dentist was pretty busy, nothing worked.

As Priscilla's sixteenth birthday approached, the queen said to the king with tears in her eyes, "I am at my wits' end. We have tried everything we could think of, and nothing has worked." She sighed sadly. "Our daughter is awful. She will never be a good successor to the throne."

The king nodded sadly. "And no one will ever want to marry her," he added, "even for half the kingdom. Besides, she would never accept anyone as a husband anyway."

"Before we give up, maybe we should consult our council once more," suggested the queen. "Perhaps someone has thought of a new idea we can try."

And that's what they did. All the royal councilors gathered in the royal meeting hall to offer their advice on this vexing situation. They murmured knowledge-ably and scratched their heads wisely, but no one could think of anything to say. After sixteen years, they were all out of ideas.

Eventually everyone realized that somebody would

have to say something. One of the older councilors
cleared his throat. He was retiring soon and felt he
could take a little risk. "Ahem!" He glared around the
room until all eyes were upon him and began, "Let us
approach this problem practically. For sixteen years,
we have been racking our brains to determine how to
make Princess Priscilla more pleasant. Perhaps we
should approach this dilemma from another angle:
when is the princess most pleasant?"

This was a difficult question. The princess was sel-
dom in a good mood. Finally, after a lot of head
scratching, one councilor said brightly, "The princess
seemed to be in a good mood when I saw her yesterday. . . ." Then he stopped and fidgeted uncomfortably.

"Well, what was she doing?" prompted the elder
councilor.

"She was . . . um . . . twisting the royal cat's tail."
The councilor wished he had kept his thoughts to
himself.

"Yes, well, thank you," grumbled the elder. "That
wasn't exactly what I was looking for."

"Oh, what's the use?" cried the distraught queen.
"Priscilla is only pleasant when she is sleeping!"

"Aha!" exclaimed the elder. "That is interesting.

Sleep is known to have curative and soothing powers. Maybe all the princess needs is a nice long sleep!" He looked around the room, very pleased with himself.

"What do you mean?" asked the king uncertainly. "Priscilla sleeps quite well, even if the bed is never made to her satisfaction."

"When I say a long sleep," explained the elder, "I mean a *really* long sleep—one that may last for years, if necessary."

"For years?" the queen looked nervous. "How is that possible?"

"Well, we could have the court magician cast a spell that would make the princess sleep until her temperament . . . ah . . . shall we say . . . mellows."

"I guess that might work," the king said slowly. He looked at the queen for her reaction.

"What if she never mellows?" the concerned queen asked. "We can't just let her sleep forever."

The elder pondered this question for a while and then exclaimed, "I have it! The spell will work until either the princess becomes pleasant and happy or until one hundred years have passed. If she is still sleeping after one hundred years, a prince will find and kiss her, ending the spell."

"We will have to think about this for a while," said the queen. "No matter how terrible she is, Priscilla is still our daughter, and we must do what is best for her."

On that note, the relieved council dispersed and the king and queen retired to their chambers.

After months of thinking and watching Priscilla gleefully reduce everyone around her to tears by both cruel words and cruel actions, the sad parents concluded that a long sleep was Priscilla's only hope.

Once they reached that decision, the king and queen had to find a way to carry it out. After consulting the court magician, they decided to throw Priscilla a sweet-sixteen party. They would present her with an enchanted spindle as one of her gifts. The careless princess was sure to prick herself, unleashing the spell.

On the day of her birthday, Priscilla had a great time. She yelled at all five of the maids who helped her get ready, pulled their hair, and made them change her dress and hairstyle twenty times. On the way to the ballroom, she tripped the servants who were carrying trays of food for the dining table, then laughed heartily while they scrambled to pick up the broken dishes and clean up the food. She kicked her pet dog hard enough to send it flying across the room and snipped the blossoms off all the flower arrangements.

During the party she continued to enjoy herself. While dancing, she stomped on her partners' feet with her spike heals, which she wore specifically for that purpose. When all the guests in their fancy clothes sat down to dinner, Priscilla began to spill red wine and throw food at everybody seated at her table.

The guests were horrified, but said nothing. After all, she was the princess, and it was her birthday. The king and queen sat helplessly and watched while their daughter tormented the honored guests. They knew that if anyone reproached Priscilla, she would throw a tantrum.

Finally, the time for opening gifts arrived. Priscilla ran to the pile of beautifully wrapped packages and began ripping bows and paper. As she unwrapped each present, she made fun of it and of the person who gave it. Naturally, nothing was good enough for her, and she did not fail to let everyone know it. Eventually she opened the spindle.

"A spindle!" Priscilla exclaimed haughtily. "Who ever heard of a princess spinning?! I certainly don't intend to spend my time on such a stupid activity." She sneered at her guests, and then a cruel smile crept across her face. "But I think I will make good use of this sharp point. Yes, indeed." Priscilla smirked. "It will help me make the servants move faster!"

Examining her new weapon, Priscilla brushed the sharp point with her finger. "Ouch!" she cried as she pricked herself. "Oh, yes, this will do just fine." She nodded with satisfaction. Then she nodded again more slowly, and the nod was accompanied by a large yawn. A few minutes later, Priscilla was fast asleep.

If the guests thought this behavior strange, they did not mention it. They were only too happy to say their good-byes and tiptoe out of the palace. Most of them had come to the party out of respect for the king and the queen, and while they pitied the poor couple, the guests did not want to spend any more time with the unpleasant princess than was absolutely necessary.

After the guests left, the king and queen placed their daughter in a tower just outside the castle wall, thinking that a prince was more likely to kiss her if he did not have to go through the whole palace to reach her. The queen put the spindle near the bed, as the sight of it made her too sad to keep it in the castle. The king and queen made sure Priscilla was comfortably and beautifully dressed, that the room was warm and clean, and they visited her every day.

As time passed, fewer people remembered Priscilla, and the tower in the wood became the center of many legends. The only true thing people remembered was Priscilla's great beauty. People added new elements to the story, creating fairies and jealous witches to make it more interesting. Someone even insisted that the princess was cursed because one fairy felt snubbed when she was not invited to the birthday party! And so the sleeping princess became more and more mysterious, until no one remembered how nasty Priscilla had been.

About one hundred years after Priscilla went to sleep, a prince was riding through the forest around the walls of the old castle. He had heard many stories about the beautiful and mysterious sleeping princess and, as he was rather conceited, he was sure that she was meant for him. He spent days wandering through the forest, hoping to glimpse the tower. The thorny branches tore at his clothes and skin. He and his horse were tired and hungry, but the prince was determined to accomplish his mission (and the horse did not have a choice).

One morning he spied the tower, which was lit by the rising sun. The prince hardly noticed the next few hours as he hacked his way through the brush; he was busy imagining what the princess would look like and composing what he would say to her. When the prince finally reached the tower, he found the door open. He flew up the curving stairway, breathless with anticipation. The stairs ended abruptly, and suddenly, the prince burst into a big room, in the middle of which the princess was sleeping on a large, luxurious bed.

The prince stopped and stared. He even pinched himself to make sure he was not dreaming. Until this moment, he realized, he had not been completely convinced that all the stories he'd heard were true. His knees grew weak, and he had to hold on to the wall to keep from falling down.

The princess was as breathtakingly beautiful as he had imagined her: for once her face was relaxed and not screwed up in a scowl. Her many curls spilled onto the pillow, framing her face, and her clothes were very becoming. That century-old fashion was just coming back into style. Once the prince reclaimed his wits, he slowly approached the bed, kissed Priscilla reverently, stepped back, and waited to see whether the enchanted princess would wake up, as legend said she would.

The story was true. Slowly, Priscilla opened her eyes and stretched. Then she looked up and saw the prince gazing at her with love in his eyes.

Without a second thought, she reached up and slapped the prince across his glowing, unsuspecting face. You see, Priscilla was not a morning person. The poor astonished prince stumbled and fell backwards, and all the words he'd composed flew out of his head. This was certainly not what he'd expected.

"What in the world do you think you're doing?" Priscilla demanded haughtily. "How dare you barge into my room and kiss me?! Guards! Guards!" As Priscilla's smooth forehead wrinkled with rage, her large, blue eyes narrowed with hostility, and her round cheeks flushed an angry red, her beautiful face turned downright ugly.

The flabbergasted prince crawled backwards toward the door, rolled down the stairs, jumped on his horse, and galloped away. He never told anyone what happened. He was sure no one would believe him—or that anyone who did would laugh at him for the rest of his life. One thing he did know for sure: he would be a lot more careful about whom he kissed in the future!

Meanwhile Priscilla was becoming unhappier by

the second. She soon realized that she was not in her room in the castle, and that no one was rushing to answer her call. In her anger, she climbed off the bed and began stomping around the room. She flung a chair out the window, ripped the curtains, and kicked the night table. Then she noticed the spindle that her unhappy mother had left by the bed. The enraged princess grabbed the spindle and aimed it at the window. As she did so, one of the spindle's sharp ends pricked Priscilla's hand. Unfortunately for Priscilla, one hundred years had not erased the spindle's magic, and she began to feel very sleepy. She barely had time to climb back into bed before her eyes closed in a deep and peaceful slumber.

Here ends the real story of Sleeping Beauty. As far as I know, she still sleeps in her tower in the forest, still beautiful, and still unmellowed.

The Obsolete Dragon

BY CAROLE G. VOGEL

We dragons don't leave our caves anymore. There's no reason to leave, nowhere to go. When I was a young, strong dragon, I was needed. You see, back then, young women did not choose their own husbands. Their fathers told them whom to marry. So desperate maidens hired me and other dragons to fight their unwanted suitors. I was in such demand, I painted my scales occasionally so no one thought it strange that one dragon was getting into so many fights. Green is my natural color, but you should have seen me when I was purple—very royal! And yellow was fun for a while.

I remember well one beautiful lady in distress: Maid Gwendolyn. I can see her standing before me now as though the whole thing happened only yesterday.

"Sir Dragon, I need your help," she pleaded. "My father has promised me to Sir Grimbald, but I can't marry him!"

"Why not?" I asked.

"People say he already has a wife in another kingdom," she replied. "Besides, I love another knight. Sir Dudley is his name. Please, Sir Dragon, I want you to fight Sir Grimbald and defeat him."

"For a fee, I will be delighted to help you, my lady," I said.

"Name your price," she responded.

"One hundred gallons of kerosene," I replied. "As you know, my breath has no fire without kerosene."

"Agreed," she said without bargaining. "But after you defeat Sir Grimbald, I want you to fight my knight, Sir Dudley, and let him defeat you. If my plan succeeds and I marry Sir Dudley, I will double your fee."

I readily agreed. She told me her plan, we worked out the details, and then she left.

One cannot fight if one's opponent does not know

that there is to be a battle. So I went from inn to inn and said terrible things about Sir Grimbald.

"Sir Grimbald is a toad-eating, good-for-nothing, cow-stealing liar!" I yelled at the first inn. My words upset no one, so I knew the knight was not there.

At the next inn I called out, "Sir Grimbald is an egg-sucking, chicken-hearted, snaggle-toothed thief!" Again, no one became angry. I traveled onward.

At the third inn I shouted, "Sir Grimbald is a flop-eared, yellow-bellied, bowlegged glob of chicken fat!" This time someone responded.

"Who dares to insult me?" cried an angry knight.

"'Tis I, the fire-breathing, death-defying, fearless green dragon."

"You are an overgrown swamp lizard," the knight sneered. "With one hand tied behind my back, I could reduce you to a pile of greasy green scales. Go back to your cave before I snuff your flame forever." Then he turned away and picked up a glass of ale.

"I believe you are afraid to battle a dragon," I said.

The knight spun around and glared at me. "Take that back or fight to the death!" he demanded.

I blew enough smoke to fill the room. "I'll see you Tuesday at daybreak in front of the vine-covered castle."

I spent the next few days preparing. I practiced terrible roars, blew smoke rings, and rehearsed my victory speech at least fifty times.

News of the coming battle spread quickly. As the sun rose on Tuesday, hundreds of people lined the battle green near the vine-covered castle. Maid Gwendolyn sat beside her father under a large tree.

At one end of the green stood Sir Grimbald, looking evil and mean. The people shouted and hissed at him.

Sir Grimbald shook his fist at them, then mounted his horse. I stood at the other end of the green, handsome and dignified. I nodded toward the people and blew perfect rings of green smoke.

"Hurrah!" the people cheered. "Squash the evil knight."

"Let the fight begin!" called the referee.

"Gra-a-agh!" I roared like thunder and raced across the green.

Sir Grimbald charged and met me in the center. With a shrill cry, he thrust his lance at my side. It bounced off.

Sir Grimbald challenged me again. This time he swung a battle-ax at my neck, but the weapon broke in two when it struck my hard scales.

Sir Grimbald attacked once more. Waving a mighty club, he yelled, "Prepare to die, dragon!" He aimed the club between my eyes. Flames leaped from my mouth and turned the club to ash.

"Enough of this play," I decided.

Billowing black smoke and roaring my loudest roar, I attacked. I knocked Sir Grimbald from his horse and backed him against a tree. As I was about to make a spectacular end of him, he ruined the show. With a cry of defeat, he dropped to the ground. He crawled from his armor, dashed under my belly, and disappeared into the crowd.

And then Maid Gwendolyn stole the show. "Oh, Father, how can I marry such a coward?" she cried. Her chin trembled, and tears streamed down her face.

"Dear daughter, you are right," said her father. "I must find someone more worthy of your hand."

Before Maid Gwendolyn's father could continue, I interrupted. "Excuse me, sir, but there is no need to find another suitor for your daughter. She now belongs to me."

"Preposterous!" her father shouted. "You have no right to her!"

"But I do. I won the battle. Maid Gwendolyn is my

prize." I grabbed the young maiden and held her to my chest.

"Help! Save me!" she screamed.

Maid Gwendolyn's father shouted to the crowd. "If any man can defeat this dragon, he may marry my daughter."

The people looked at each other nervously. Would anyone accept the challenge?

"I will fight the dragon," called a voice from the middle of the crowd.

People stared as the challenger marched forward. "It's Sir Dudley!" they cried. "He has saved many a lady in distress."

I put Maid Gwendolyn down and charged Sir Dudley. Our battle was quickly fought. The knight thrust a gleaming sword toward my heart. I shifted my body a bit, and the sword slid harmlessly under my arm, puncturing a pouch of red dye hidden there. As the dye leaked to the ground, I pretended to be gravely wounded. I roared a few pitiful roars, belched a cloud of steam, rolled over, and played dead. What a performance!

"My hero!" Maid Gwendolyn called as she rushed onto the battle green and into Sir Dudley's arms.

"Hurrah!" shouted the people.

The men congratulated Sir Dudley. The women gathered around me and pretended to examine my fallen body. In whispers, they praised my grand acting.

"What color will you paint your scales next?" asked one young maiden.

"What name will you fight under?" asked another.

"How much will you charge to help me avoid a terrible marriage?" asked a third.

After the people left the green, I crept silently to my cave. At the entrance I found two hundred gallons of kerosene, just as Gwendolyn had promised.

"Thank you!" read a large note attached to them. "I will tell all my friends about you. Love, Gwendolyn."

Alas, as time passed, fewer and fewer young maidens needed my help. Maidens had more say about their marriages. Why today, they even choose their own husbands! Modern women have no use for dragons, so I, and all other dragons, have become obsolete.

But I don't want to sit in this dark, drafty cave blowing smoke rings for the rest of my life. That's why I'm opening a school. I'll train young dragons for dramatic roles in video games and movies. With my acting talent, I know I'll be a smashing success!

The Frog Princess

BY RITA SCHLACHTER

I am a frog. A frog princess. And like any princess, I've always dreamed of a handsome prince sweeping me off my feet.

Well, one sunny afternoon while I was basking in the warmth on my favorite lily pad, I looked up . . . and there he was, leading his horse to my pond for a drink. He was tall, with sparkling pond-green eyes and mud-brown hair. My heart started beating double time. I became so tongue-tied I couldn't catch the pesky fly buzzing around my head. The prince knelt down and dipped his cupped hands into the water. Suddenly . . .

"My ring!" he shrieked. A gold-and-ruby band

sank to the bottom of the pond, well out of his reach.

This was my big chance. Splash! I leaped onto the bank beside the prince. "Perhaps I can help."

"You're a frog," said the prince.

"A frog princess," I said.

"How can a frog help a prince?"

"I can swim."

"Then you must save my ruby ring, because I can't swim," said the prince. "That ring has been in my family for generations. As the eldest son, I received it as a sign that I will, in time, be the next king."

"I will retrieve your ring on one condition," I said. (I know that a reward shouldn't be the reason for doing a good deed. But who knew when a prince would stop by my pond again? I couldn't let this opportunity slip by.)

"What more could a frog want than a pond, a lily pad, and a few juicy flies?" asked the prince.

"A companion," I answered. "You must agree to marry me."

"You're a frog!" exclaimed the prince.

"I am really a princess," I explained. "An angry witch turned me into a frog when my father refused to let her snip one of his prize roses. You must always be careful what you say to a witch. They have terrible tempers."

"That's awful," said the prince. "But you're a frog now, and I could never marry a frog."

I looked in the pond. "Shoo, little fish. Don't eat that ruby ring."

The prince splashed his hand into the water to scare the fish away. "I could never stand on the castle balcony and wave to the people with a frog wife standing beside me. I could never sit next to a frog wife in a dining room filled with important dignitaries. No, never."

"Oh, dear," I said, looking at the swirling water. "I think your ruby ring is sinking into the mud."

"Okay, okay, I'll marry you. Just save my ruby ring!" cried the prince.

I jumped into the pond and returned in a flash, with the ring in my mouth. The ungrateful prince snatched the ring, leaped on his horse, and galloped for the castle. I immediately took off after him. Of course, I needed a lot more time to get there.

Once inside the castle, I hopped up and down the halls until I heard a familiar voice. It was coming from the dining room. I peeked through the space under the door and saw my prince sitting at the table with his father, the king.

I tapped on the door and called, "Handsome prince, let me in."

"Who is that?" asked the king.

"A frog," groaned the prince.

"A frog princess," I corrected him.

"Why are you here?" asked the king.

"I retrieved the prince's ruby ring from the pond. In return the prince promised to marry me."

"Is this true?" asked the king. The prince only moaned. "In that case," the king said, "you'd better let her in."

The prince dejectedly opened the door and then hurried back to his seat. I hopped into the room.

"I know I will make the prince a very good wife," I told the king.

"A prince cannot marry a frog," said the prince.

"A frog princess," I corrected him again.

"You cannot go back on your word," said the honorable king.

I leaped onto the back of the throne and said, "Kiss me."

"A prince does not kiss a frog," said the unhappy prince.

"A frog princess." I was getting tired of repeating myself.

Then I stretched up on my back legs so I could reach the prince. I noticed he closed his eyes, wrinkled his nose, and held his breath. Our lips met. *POOF!*

The handsome prince turned into a frog! A very handsome frog prince.

"It all happened one day while I was sitting on my favorite lily pad," I explained as the frog prince and I hopped back to the pond. "A fairy godmother was flying by, and she dropped her magic wand into the pond. Of course I jumped in after it. She wanted to reward me. Unfortunately, she could not turn me back into a beautiful princess. But she did grant me one wish!"

Rudy and the Prince

BY LISA HARKRADER

It's once upon a time, around five in the morning. The vines are slick with dew, and I'm hanging from the side of the castle, trying to get a foothold so I can climb up into the tower. It's not exactly what I had in mind when I took this jester job. Prince Charming's down below, safe and snug on his horse.

"Hurry, Rudy," he tells me. "And keep it quiet when you get inside. Mother's a light sleeper."

Yeah, right. Let *him* try scaling a wall with bells on his shoes and see how quiet *he* can be.

The prince has enrolled in the Enchanted Forest

Academy of Fashion Design. He hasn't told his parents yet. They have their hearts set on him rescuing a princess and living happily ever after. They're throwing a ball tonight so he can meet all the eligible young women in the kingdom.

The prince isn't interested. "I'll get married someday," he keeps telling me, "but right now I need to focus on my career."

"Hey, tell *them,* not me," I say.

The prince shakes his head. "You know my folks," he says. "They'd never understand."

The prince figures he'd look pretty suspicious prancing through the castle with fabric swatches and a sketchbook. So he stashes his design equipment under the mattress in the tower guest room. Every morning we ride out the front gate—the prince in full armor, me in this stupid jester getup. Then we circle around to the back of the castle. He parks himself safely in the trees while I shinny up the tower to get his stuff. I end up swinging from vines before the sunrise, like an insomniac Tarzan in tights.

"Well, *I* can't climb up there wearing this tin can," the prince complains as he looks thoughtfully at his breastplate. "Maybe I should design a suit of armor that is spear-resistant yet comfortable, and at the same time fashionable and easy to care for. What do you think, Rudy? Something in a wrinkle-free aluminum knit?"

Whatever. I climb over the balcony, jingle into the guest room, and grope under the mattress until I find the Prince's stuff. Then I slide back down the castle wall. The prince secures his things, and we set off, looking like any other prince and his jester. Well . . . except for the sewing basket and bolt of lavender chiffon bouncing behind the prince's saddle.

We've been riding awhile when the prince says, "Rudy, we're lost."

No kidding. We've passed the same gingerbread house three times. It's not my fault. I wanted to stay on the interstate, but His Charmingness insisted he knew a shortcut through the woods. He's in a big hurry to start his final project.

"That looks like a castle." The prince points through the trees. "It's pretty run-down, but maybe somebody can give us directions."

Not likely. It seems to be naptime at the castle. We climb up into the tower and find a princess snoring beside a spinning wheel. She's got a scar on her finger, and there are dried bloodstains on the carpet. I shake her shoulder, but she doesn't stir.

"She's out cold," I say. "Maybe we should take her to a hospital."

"Not in *that* gown, Rudy. It's at least a hundred years out of date. And it's falling apart." The prince chews on his lip and studies the princess. "I'd say she's about a size twelve, wouldn't you?"

How should I know? Do I look like Calvin Klein? Sheesh!

While I try to revive the princess, the prince dashes down to his horse. He returns carrying the polka-dotted dress he designed in his Intro to Party Wear class. He lays it out alongside the princess.

"Perfect," he says. "She'll be stunning."

He plucks the cobwebs from the poor girl and drapes the dress over the spinning wheel. Then he smoothes her bangs, which got a little mussed while I was performing CPR, and kisses her. They don't call him Prince Charming for nothing.

The princess's eyes flutter open. "Boy," she says, "am I starved. I must've slept through breakfast."

The girl's parents barrel into the room.

Her father slaps Prince Charming on the back. "You saved her, my boy!"

Her mother smiles. "You know what this means, of course."

"It means we've gotta go. If the dress gets soiled, hand-wash it in cold water with a mild detergent." The prince swings his sewing basket over his shoulder. "Come on, Rudy. We're late."

"Aren't you forgetting something?" her father calls after us. "Tradition requires that you . . ."

We don't hear the rest. As I said, the prince is hot to get started on his project.

We haven't ridden long when we stumble across another snoozing lady. She's lying in a glass case in the backyard of a little cottage. Seven really short guys are gazing at her and sniffling.

"Rudy, look!" The prince swings down from his horse. "The color!"

"She *is* turning kind of blue around the lips."

"Not that." The prince lifts the lid of the case. "Her gown! Have you ever seen such deep crimson?" He leans in for a better look and falls—elbows first—onto the lady's stomach.

The lady gags and coughs up a big apple chunk. She blinks at the prince and says, "Get off me, you oaf."

"Sorry." The prince wriggles out of the case. "We

seem to be lost. We're looking for the Enchanted Forest Academy of Fashion Design."

"Well, it's not in here." She sits up and straightens her dress. "Turn right at the end of our driveway and get on the interstate. You can't miss it."

The prince kisses the lady's hand, then turns and leaps onto his horse.

"Hey, mister," says the shortest guy, "ain't you supposed to take Ms. White with you?"

"No can do," says the prince. "We're already late."

We make it to the academy without meeting any more dozing damsels. The prince reveals his final project idea to me during his formalwear workshop. I'm standing on a chair wearing a ball gown while the prince hems the skirt. I've been his model ever since he started this little fashion adventure. Sports apparel wasn't so bad. I got a great pair of cross-trainers out of the deal. But I never want to relive that ladies' swimwear business again.

"My theory," he says, "is that a well-designed gown and the right accessories can turn any young lady into a princess. This ball my folks are throwing tonight will be my chance prove it."

"Count me out," I say. "I'm too hairy for the strapless look."

"Not you. No hard feelings, buddy, but my grade took a dive when you modeled that bikini." The prince turns me so he can hem the back. "You know that chambermaid we pass every morning—the one who dumps the garbage?"

"Cinderella?"

"Yeah. Here's the plan." He finishes stitching and snips the thread. "I rented a carriage. Budget Buggy needs it back by midnight, though, so Cinderella will have to leave the ball early. Your job is to convince her to come in the first place."

He rummages around on his worktable and pulls out one of his sister's old ballet costumes. "Wear this. But lose the jester hat. I'll fix you up with a tiara or something. And a wand, of course. Wave it and—*poof!* —you change an eggplant into a handsome carriage."

"An eggplant?"

"Eggplant, pumpkin, whatever's growing in the garden. Then—*poof!*—the dress appears."

"Poof, huh? And she's not gonna notice when I run off and fetch the dress and carriage stashed behind the garage?"

"Tell her to close her eyes. Gee whiz, Rudy, do I

have to think of everything?"

"I've got a better idea. Give her the dress and an invitation to the ball, and just ask her to help you out."

The prince rolls his eyes. "Be sensible, Rudy. She'd never believe Prince Charming designs formalwear."

But she'll buy a fairy godmother with razor stubble?

Next thing I know, I'm standing in the alley behind Cinderella's house wearing a tutu that won't zip all the way. Cinderella comes out to dump the trash.

"Close your eyes," I say, "and you'll get a big surprise."

"You're gonna get a big surprise, buddy, if you don't get out of my yard."

"Look, Cinderella, I'm just doing my job. There's a carriage around the corner. I've got this dress. Why don't you go change, and I'll take you to the ball?"

Her eyes narrow. "Are you asking me out?"

"Look, just put on the dress. I'll explain on the way."

Cinderella is a pretty good sport once I spill the whole story. "Hey, I understand," she says. "I've got dreams of my own. But I can't guarantee I'll be able to dance in glass slippers."

Not to worry. Cinderella makes a big splash at the

party. Prince Charming sure knows how to put together a ball gown. He could use a little help in the small-talk department, though. He spends most of the night dragging Cinderella from guest to guest, making introductions.

"I'd like you to meet Cinderella," he tells them. "She's wearing a classic gown that achieves a striking balance between brilliant glamour and quiet elegance. The strapless bodice of gold brocade is set off by the deep blue, full-cut velvet skirt. A single strand of pearls completes the ensemble."

Oh, brother.

He gets some pretty funny looks from the party guests, but his folks are thrilled—especially when he starts scribbling notes for his project report. They think he's writing down Cinderella's phone number. Then the band takes a break, and we hear the clock bonging away in the tower.

Cinderella glances at her watch. "Oh, man! I gotta get over to Budget Buggy." She grabs her purse and heads for the door. The king runs after her, but all he finds is one of her shoes at the bottom of the steps.

The next morning there's a big commotion in the throne room. The princess we found in the tower is yawning while her parents holler at the seven little guys from the forest. Ms. White's inching toward the door. Suddenly, the king's men march in carrying Cinderella.

"The shoe fits," says one of the men.

The queen looks like she's going to pass out.

"What's going on?" asks the prince.

The king clears his throat. "Son, it seems you are engaged to marry all three of these women."

"Marry?" Cinderella shakes herself free of the guards. "Like I'm gonna meet this guy one day and marry him the next! Are you people living in a fairy tale?"

The king looks flustered. "Son, you can't go around rescuing maidens willy-nilly and then leaving them. Certain things are expected of you."

"Quite right," says the queen. "I met your father when he climbed my hair to rescue me from a tower. We've lived happily ever after. That's all we want for you, dear."

"But it's not what I want, Mother." The prince pulls his sketchbook out from under his breastplate and turns to the page with Cinderella's dress on it. "See?"

"Oh, my." The queen leafs through the sketchbook.

"You did these?"

The king looks over the queen's shoulder. "You've got quite a talent, son."

"I don't mean to hurt your feelings," says the prince, "but I can't live happily ever after without my design work. I must finish my studies at the academy." He turns to the three ladies. "Sorry for the mistake."

"No big deal," says Ms. White. "I've been cleaning up after these dwarves for months. They're sweet and they'd do anything for me, but not one of them has figured out how to take his socks off right side out. And replacing empty toilet paper rolls? Forget it. Look, Prince, you seem like a nice guy, and I appreciate the Heimlich maneuver yesterday, but I don't need another man in my life right now. No offense."

"Me neither," says the yawning princess. "I've been cooped up in that castle for a hundred years. I thought I'd take the summer off and backpack through Europe."

So the three ladies head off to make their own tales. The prince begins measuring his mother for a new dress, and the king starts a guest list for the prince's graduation party. In the spirit of the moment, I kick my shoes into the fireplace. Good-bye, jingle bells. And while I'm at it, the stupid hat goes, too. I lace up my cross-trainers, thinking everybody's finally going to live happily ever after.

Monday morning the prince and I are headed for the fashion academy when the prince stops suddenly.

"Rudy, take a look at the girl with the basket. I don't believe it!"

Me neither. She's chatting with a wolf.

"What is that awful red thing she's wearing? It doesn't flatter her figure at all. But you know, with some gathering below the waist and maybe a three-quarter length sleeve...."

Goldy Locks

BY TIMOTHY TOCHER

Papa Bear fixed his beady eyes on the car pulling out of the driveway. He'd just seen a little girl with a backpack and a man in a business suit leave the house. The woman backed her station wagon over the edge of the lawn and roared off.

Papa Bear was sure the house was finally empty. He woofed softly, and his son was instantly by his side, sticking his nose through the bushes.

Mama Bear was worried. "Please, honey, let's go back over the mountain. I'm sure we can find a good den for the winter. Maybe we missed a spot."

"Missed a spot? Those bulldozers have knocked down so many trees that there's nowhere left to hide.

99

Once they decided to build that highway, our home was doomed," Papa Bear answered.

"But, honey," Mama Bear protested, "we can't live with people."

"We can't live without them, either. They've taken our home; now I'm taking one of theirs."

"Think of Baby Bear," Mama Bear tried again. "It's not safe for him to spend the winter in somebody's basement. What if we're found?"

"People aren't sensible like bears," Papa Bear assured her. "They won't come back to this den until nightfall. By then we'll be deep in hibernation in the ground under their den. They won't even know we're there."

Papa Bear would have been surprised if he'd been watching the back of the house at that moment. Goldy Locks had left the house, but she hadn't gone to her bus stop. She, too, had been waiting for her parents to leave. As soon as her mom drove away, she snuck back to the house and entered through the back door, which she had left unlocked.

Goldy liked school and had never played hooky before. But today she had an important reason. She belonged to the Hair Raising Book Club, and just yesterday she'd received the latest book in the mail.

Return of the Monsters #4 was sure to be the best one yet, and she couldn't wait to read it. She had loved all the *Monster* books. How could she be expected to sit in school when her new book was waiting at home? Besides, her classmate, Mary Contrary, had probably read the whole book last night and would be blabbing the ending to everyone.

Goldy raced up to her room, forgetting to lock the back door behind her. She passed through her bedroom, grabbed the book from her nightstand, and ducked into the crawlspace behind her clothes closet. She kept a flashlight there especially for reading scary stories.

"If you know so much about people, how are we going to get into their den?" asked Mama Bear.

"People are stupid—that's how. They have so many holes leading into their dens that someone always leaves one open. Let's go check."

The three bears ambled across the lawn and onto the front porch. To Mama Bear's relief, everything was locked up tight. Papa Bear headed around back, however, and soon found the door Goldy had left open.

"Come on!" he urged the others. As soon as they were inside, he closed the door with a swipe of a paw.

Upstairs, Goldy jumped at the sound but decided it was just her imagination. She returned to her book. The monsters were digging their way out of the coal mine in which they'd been buried in *Return of the Monsters #3*.

"How do we get to the basement?" asked Mama Bear. She hated being in this house; it smelled strange. She wanted to hide.

"We've got all day," replied Papa Bear. Let's explore first. I've always wanted to see one of these human dens, and now's our chance."

"Yeah, Pop, let's check it out!" cried Baby Bear. "If you hold your nose, it's not bad in here."

"We'll start at the top and work our way down," commanded Papa Bear. "Follow me!" He bounded down the hall and up the stairs. He loved the way his sharp claws dug into the carpet.

Baby Bear jumped onto the railing and shinnied up until he banged his head on the knob at the top.

His mother lifted him down and gently prodded him along the hall. Papa Bear ran through the first open doorway—into the bathroom. When his feet hit the tile floor, he slid all the way across the room and bounced off the toilet.

He was still rubbing the lump on his head when his son crashed into him from behind. Only cautious Mama Bear came in without falling.

Goldy jumped again in her crawlspace. This was the scariest book yet. The spooky story and being home alone were really getting to her. She could swear she'd heard noises coming from the bathroom.

"What's this room for, Pop? Why's the floor slippery?

Papa Bear looked around. Then he spotted the pool of water in the toilet. "Uh . . . this is where people drink, Son. They don't even have to go outside."

He lapped some water from the bowl, then moved aside so Mama Bear and Baby Bear could have a taste.

"I don't smell any fish in it," said Papa Bear. "Too bland."

"Not cold enough," said Mama Bear. "Give me a fresh mountain stream any day."

"I think it's great! Water right in your den! People have it made," said Baby Bear.

He reached out his paw and touched the handle. "What's this for, Pop?" He pulled it down. The rush of noise and water scared all three bears. But it shocked Goldy most of all.

"Oh no, there *is* someone here! What if it's the

monsters? Maybe this time they've returned to my house!" She flipped through the book and was happy to see no mention of her house. It looked like the monsters would terrorize a mall this time.

Goldy was terrified, but she reminded herself that no one knew she was there. Maybe if she stayed still, whatever was out there (using her toilet—yuck!) would go away. She shut off her flashlight and sat miserably in the dark, hugging her knees.

The startled bears were skidding around the bathroom, their claws scrabbling on the tile. Then they began to calm down.

"Awesome, Pop! That handle makes a little waterfall so the water's always fresh." He pushed the lever again.

"Please stop doing that!" begged Mama Bear.

"What is wrong with this person?" wondered Goldy. "Or are there two people?"

Baby Bear was bouncing around the bathroom, cuffing every handle and lever he could find. When he started the shower, all three bears gaped in amazement.

"Indoor rain! I can't believe it! People are so smart!"

"You mean so dumb, Son. They have everything from outdoors here in their den, yet they go off and leave it empty all day."

"Let's check some other rooms," said Baby as he raced down the hall to Goldy's bedroom.

Baby looked around in awe. He didn't know what to make of Goldy's television or CD player. But her bed looked so soft, he scrambled up on it. Then he froze.

Leaning against the pillow was a smaller version of—himself! He woofed at the teddy bear, but it didn't respond. He was batting it gently with his paw when his parents shuffled into the room.

"Look, Pop, they like us! Here's a fake cub that looks almost like me."

Papa Bear was amazed too. "I told you: they have everything from outside in here—even bears. But none of it's as good. That bear just sits there all day. What good is he?"

Goldy was becoming almost as curious as she was frightened. She heard woofing noises, shuffling footsteps, groaning bedsprings. What was going on?

She crept across the crawlspace and put her eye against a crack in the door. She could see part of her bed through the open closet door. Sitting on it was the cutest bear cub she had ever seen! It looked a lot like Teddy, her dear stuffed bear. Not that she still played with stuffed animals. She was far too grown-up for that. It was just that Teddy had been with her as long as she could remember, so she kept him around.

Goldy was so excited to see a bear cub that she almost burst out of the crawlspace for a closer look. But just then her view was blocked by something big and hairy. There was a grown bear, too!

As Papa Bear crossed the room, Goldy caught sight of Mama Bear standing timidly in the doorway. Three bears! The whole situation seemed strangely familiar to Goldy. Maybe she had read something similar in a Hair-Raising book.

Baby Bear bounded from the bed into the closet. Goldy thought he had spotted her, but he was just exploring.

"Pop, what are all these for?" He pointed to the dozens of hangers holding Goldy's clothes.

"Be happy we have hair, Son. People have to use all this stuff to protect themselves from the weather."

Mama Bear stamped her paw angrily.

"Did we come here to find a den or not? We're wasting the whole day, and we don't even know if there's a spot for us here. I'm going downstairs to look in the basement."

"Come on, Son. Mama is right. We've had our fun,

but we still need someplace to spend the winter. Follow me."

Papa Bear ambled out of the closet, through the bedroom, and down the stairs. Baby Bear reluctantly followed, and Mama Bear brought up the rear.

When they were gone, Goldy crept from her hiding place and listened at the top of the stairs. The basement door was ajar, and she heard the bears squeeze through and barrel down the steps.

The three bears stumbled into a huge room packed with old toys, broken furniture, bicycles, and piles of books and magazines.

Mama Bear rubbed her paws on the concrete floor. "We can't dig into this. This is even harder than the rest of the house. We can't stay here."

Papa Bear was ashamed. He'd been sure that there was bare earth under the people's house. But there was not one corner into which he could dig. He knew he and Mama Bear could survive a winter with little food and shelter, but he wasn't so sure about Baby Bear.

Meanwhile, Goldy kept leaning further and further through the basement door, trying to see what the bears were up to. At last she leaned too far, and down the stairs she tumbled.

The noise made Papa Bear and Mama Bear rear up and growl fiercely as they jumped between Baby Bear and the steps. But when they saw the little girl, they dropped down on all fours.

For a moment no one moved. Goldy wasn't hurt, just a little dazed. Baby Bear squeezed between his protective parents and nudged Goldy with his snout. His cold nose tickled her, and she laughed. Baby Bear nudged her again. She reached out slowly, keeping one eye on his parents, and scratched him behind the ear. He loved it and pressed against her fingers for more.

"Let's leave. This one is harmless, but more people may come. Let's go while we still can!" insisted Mama.

"Come on, Son. We're heading back outdoors where we belong. This whole expedition was a terrible mistake."

Goldy heard their sounds, but she had no idea what the bears were saying to each other. She only knew she'd like to scratch and cuddle Baby Bear forever.

"Mom, Pop, I love you, but this hibernation stuff is not for me. That was fine for you old bears. When you were kids there was plenty of wilderness and you could hunker down in a hole and sleep a few months away each year. But things are different now. I've got to learn how to live with people. This girl likes me, and I'd like to stay right here for the winter."

"But what will you eat?" exclaimed Mama Bear.

"People have to eat, too, and I'll bet that like everything else, they do it right in this den. The girl will take care of me—I know it. In the spring you and Dad and I will all look for a new place to live."

Goldy sensed that something exciting was about to happen. She got up slowly, and Baby Bear nuzzled her legs. Goldy didn't think bears could cry, but Mama Bear looked like she might. The two big bears trudged up the steps and were gone. Goldy heard the back door slam and she and Baby Bear were alone. She knew she must keep him—at least for the winter. But where?

Her crawlspace! It would be perfect! It was warm and dry. Her parents never went in there, and she could let Baby Bear out into her room at night.

That winter was the happiest of Goldy's life. She and Baby Bear played every night. She read him scary stories by flashlight. They snuggled together when the winter winds blew.

Mr. and Mrs. Locks were pleased to see Goldy so happy, but they were also a little worried. Her appetite seemed to have increased tremendously—the fridge was always empty. She spent a lot of time in her room, and she snored very loudly when she slept. The family doctor gave Goldy a thorough checkup and told her parents not to worry.

At school, Goldy started an ecology club. The club members picked up trash along hiking trails in the woods. They recycled bottles, cans, and newspapers and donated the money to wildlife groups.

Goldy's new interest helped her become an even better student, which made Mr. and Mrs. Locks happy and eager to help with her cause. It was too late to stop the highway construction, but they were able to persuade the builders to provide tunnels so animals could cross safely. And they helped groups in nearby communities who were trying to preserve their woodlands.

As for Mama and Papa Bear, the winter went well for them. They spent it curled up in the nature center Goldy's club had helped start.

Goldy was still haunted by a feeling that she had met these bears before. She couldn't quite recall the story, but she knew that this time it would have a happier ending.

AUTHOR BIOGRAPHIES

Lisa Harkrader, the author of "Rudy and the Prince," was in third grade when she first decided she wanted to write and illustrate books. Ever since then, she's been working hard to turn that dream into reality. She earned a B.F.A. in painting from the University of Kansas, and had stories published in *Cricket, Guideposts for Kids, Fantastic Flyer,* and *Story Friends.* She is the coauthor of *Kidding around Kansas City* and a contributing author to *A Treasury of Christmas Stories.* Lisa lives on a farm outside Tonganoxie, Kansas, with her husband and two children, Ashley and Austin.

Bruce Lansky, the author of "The Prince and the Pea," has been writing stories about clever, courageous girls for *Girls to the Rescue,* a series he also edits. This is his first story about a boy (although it does feature yet another spunky female). Bruce also enjoys writing funny poetry, some of which can be found in *Poetry Party,* and performing in school assemblies and teacher conferences. He has two grown children and currently lives with his computer near a beautiful lake in Minnesota.

V. McQuin is happily married and the mother of seven children. She lives in Cheyenne, Wyoming, and stays busy caring for her family and home-schooling her children. She enjoys reading, gardening, cross-stitching, and watching the kids grow and learn. She wrote "And So They Did" for a fairy-tale-loving daughter and had a great time doing it.

Liya Lev Oertel graduated from Brown University with degrees in psychology and visual arts. She is originally from Minsk, Byelorussia, and has lived in the United States for seventeen years. Currently, she works as an editor and lives in Minneapolis, Minnesota, with her husband, Jens. Liya has a story published in *Girls to the Rescue, Book #4.* She loves mysteries, gardening, dancing, and swimming. Liya had a lot of fun writing "The Real Story of Sleeping Beauty."

Rita Schlachter, the author of "The Frog Princess," lives in Cincinnati, Ohio, with her husband, Phil. She has one son in college, Steven, and two married daughters, Traci and Michelle. Rita has written five books and two magazine stories for children. In addition to reading and writing, Rita enjoys helping her daughter—who works with the rescue and rehabilitation of wildlife—care for injured and orphaned baby animals.

Timothy Tocher, the author of "King Midas," "Little Bad Wolf and Little Red Riding Hood," and "Goldy Locks," teaches at George Grant Mason Elementary in Tuxedo, New York. He lives with his wife, Judy, in nearby Rockland County. His humorous poems have been published in *Kids Pick the Funniest Poems, No More Homework! No More Tests!,* and in various magazines for teachers.

Denise Vega has been writing since she was a child. She currently works as a technical writer as she pursues children's writing. Denise received her B.A. in Motion Picture-Television from UCLA and her Masters in Education from Harvard University. She hopes to develop a CD ROM for kids and is currently working on a young adult novel set in 1250 A.D. Denise lives in Denver, Colorado, with her husband and two kids. She loves to camp, fish, and hike in the Rockies. Denise wrote "Jill and the Beanstalk" as a result of reading "Jack and the Beanstalk" to her kids and realizing for the first time that it's really a story about a lazy boy who is rewarded for stealing!

Carole Garbuny Vogel specializes in nonfiction for young readers. Known as the "Queen of Natural Disasters," she is the author of thirteen books, including *Shock Waves through Los Angeles: The Northridge Earthquake,* and *The Great Midwest Flood.* She has won numerous awards for her writing. Her story, "The Obsolete Dragon," earned an honorable mention in the 1996 Black Hills Writer's Competition, which received about 900 entries. Carole graduated from Kenyon College with a B.A. in biology and received an M.A.T. in elementary education from the University of Pittsburgh. She lives in Lexington, Massachusetts, with her husband and two teenage children.

The Girls to the Rescue Series

Edited by Bruce Lansky

Here are the first four collections of stories featuring heroic, clever, and determined girls from around the world. Each book contains tales about girls such as Emily, who helps a runaway slave and her baby reach safety and freedom, and Kamala, a Punjabi girl who outsmarts a pack of thieves. This series for girls ages 7 to 13 has received critical acclaim and raves from mothers and daughters alike. **$3.95**

Order # 2215   **Order # 2216**

Order # 2219   **Order # 2221**

Newfangled Fairy Tales, Book #2

Edited by Bruce Lansky

Here is the second book in the successful anthology series of entertaining fairy tales with delightfully newfangled twists. It contains ten contemporary fairy tales that will appeal to boys and girls, and includes characters such as Michelle, who desperately wants to be a princess until her wish comes true and she discovers what a pain royal life can be, and Hansel, who is so obsessed with candy that he steals Gretel's piggy bank and runs off to the Old Witch's Candy Factory.

Order # 2501 $3.95

Order Form

Qty.	Title	Author	Order No.	Unit Cost (U.S. $)	Total
	Bad Case of the Giggles	Lansky, B.	2411	$16.00	
	Miles of Smiles	Lansky, B.	2412	$16.00	
	Free Stuff for Kids	Free Stuff Editors	2190	$5.00	
	Girls to the Rescue	Lansky, B.	2215	$3.95	
	Girls to the Rescue, Book #2	Lansky, B.	2216	$3.95	
	Girls to the Rescue, Book #3	Lansky, B.	2219	$3.95	
	Girls to the Rescue, Book #5	Lansky, B.	2222	$3.95	
	Kids' Holiday Fun	Warner, P.	6000	$12.00	
	Kids' Party Games and Activities	Warner, P.	6095	$12.00	
	Kids' Pick-A-Party Book	Warner, P.	6090	$9.00	
	Kids Pick the Funniest Poems	Lansky, B.	2410	$15.00	
	New Adventures of Mother Goose	Lansky, B.	2420	$15.00	
	Newfangled Fairy Tales, Book #1	Lansky, B.	2500	$3.95	
	Newfangled Fairy Tales, Book #2	Lansky, B.	2501	$3.95	
	No More Homework! No More Tests!	Lansky, B.	2414	$8.00	
	Poetry Party	Lansky, B.	2430	$12.00	
	Young Marian's Adventures	Mooser, S.	2218	$4.50	
				Subtotal	
		Shipping and Handling, see below			
		MN residents add 6.5% sales tax			
				Total	

YES, please send me the books indicated above. Add $2.00 shipping and handling for the first book and $.50 for each additional book. Add $2.50 to total for books shipped to Canada. Overseas postage will be billed. Allow up to four weeks for delivery. Send check or money order payable to Meadowbrook Press. No cash or C.O.D.'s please. Prices subject to change without notice. **Quantity discounts available upon request.**

Send book(s) to:

Name_____

Address_____

City _____State _____ Zip _____

Telephone (_____) _____

Purchase order number (if necessary) _____

Payment via:

☐ Check or money order payable to Meadowbrook (No cash or C.O.D.'s please)
  Amount enclosed $_____

☐ Visa (for orders over $10.00 only)   ☐ MasterCard (for orders over $10.00 only)

Account # _____

Signature _____ Exp. Date _____

You can also phone us for orders of $10.00 or more at 1-800-338-2232.

A *FREE* Meadowbrook catalog is available upon request.

Mail to: Meadowbrook Press
5451 Smetana Drive, Minnetonka, MN 55343

Phone (612) 930-1100   Toll-Free 1-800-338-2232   Fax (612) 930-1940